sh

Willa Marsh was born in Somerset and lives in Devon with her husband and two Newfoundlands. Her previous three novels, *Amy Wingate's Journal*, *Facing the Music*, and *Sisters Under the Skin*, are also available from Sceptre. As Marcia Willett, she also writes well-reviewed novels published by Headline.

Praise for Willa Marsh:

'A genuine voice of our times' *The Times*

'With beautifully ironic observations and flashbacks to a mysterious past, the story has a twist in the tail so staggering that it necessitates re-reading and a strong cup of tea' *The Lady*

Praise for Marcia Willett:

'A fascinating study of character . . . A cleverly woven story with lots of human interest' *Publishing News*

'A very readable book' *Prima*

SCEPTRE

Also by Willa Marsh

Sisters Under the Skin
Facing the Music
Amy Wingate's Journal

Writing as Marcia Willett:

Looking Forward
Second Time Around
Starting Over
Hattie's Mill
The Dipper
The Courtyard
Thea's Parrot
Those Who Serve

The Quick and the Dead

WILLA MARSH

SCEPTRE

Copyright © 1999 Marcia Willett

First published in 1999 by Hodder and Stoughton
First published in paperback in 1999 by Hodder and Stoughton
A division of Hodder Headline PLC
A Sceptre Paperback

The right of Marcia Willett to be identified as the Author of
the Work has been asserted by her in accordance with the
Copyright, Designs and Patents Act 1988.

10 9 8 7 6 5 4 3 2 1

A CIP catalogue record for this book is available
from the British Library

ISBN 0 340 70800 X

Typeset by Palimpsest Book Production Limited,
Polmont, Stirlingshire
Printed and bound in Great Britain by
Mackays of Chatham PLC, Chatham, Kent

Hodder and Stoughton
A division of Hodder Headline PLC
338 Euston Road
London NW1 3BH

To Molly and Barrie

She is there again this morning, standing at the end of the drive, half hidden by the oak trees, camouflaged by the shadows. As she stares at the house her attitude is one of eagerness and longing; a desperate hunger emanates from her still, tensely focused figure. The milk van comes rattling down the lane and she turns aside swiftly, melting into the darkness of the woods.

Both Gwyneth and Olwen have seen her. Her brooding presence has alerted these two aged guardians: the present custodians of the house. From their rooms on the first floor, standing well back from the mullioned windows lest they be seen, they watch her. Their thoughts reach out to her, like invisible probes, testing and questioning. They see her disappear amongst the trees and smile gently to themselves.

Clarissa does not see her at all. She sees only the dappled shade, the gleam of the sun through the bare branches, the shadows moving on the drive; all her thoughts are turned inwards. Her face is set in unhappy lines; her arms are folded beneath her breast, hands gripping elbows.

'It isn't fair,' she mutters. 'It simply isn't *fair*.'

The clear, regular note of a bell is carried on the breeze, across the fields and into the valleys. It is time for Terce at the convent on the hill. Gwyneth and Olwen move uneasily, frowning at the pure, high call to prayer and Clarissa sighs as she turns away from the window. It is too late now to talk to Thomas about his daughter's obsession with the nuns. Easter is past and, very soon now, Megan will enter the convent as a postulant whilst she, Clarissa, will be left in this old house, miles from civilisation, with only a cripple and two old women for companionship.

'It isn't fair!' cries Clarissa – and Olwen and Gwyneth, pausing outside her bedroom door to listen, nod wisely to each other, recognising the note of frustration in her voice.

It has not always been so. In the early days Clarissa thinks she must have died and gone to heaven when she marries Thomas and moves to the house surrounded by the ancient oak wood. She first meets Thomas at a friend's house where he is staying after the death of his wife. The poor woman, apparently, has never really recovered from a series of miscarriages and now she is gone, leaving Thomas with fifteen-year-old Megan and two elderly aunts for whom to care. He is charmingly old-fashioned – courteous and gentle; considerate and sincere – and Clarissa is very taken with him. When he talks of the old Tudor house standing in the oak woodlands in the Welsh marches, of the lawns and the river and the mountains, Clarissa realises just how tired she is of the smoke and grime of London streets. He describes the house, spacious and cool and quiet, and she thinks with distaste of her cramped basement flat in Fulham. He tells her of his daughter, of pretty, charming little Megan, and she is aware of her maternal instinct – never very far from the surface – rising within her.

His hosts, behind his back so as to preserve his finer feelings, speak to her glowingly of Thomas's wealth and the nobility and lineage of his family. They have suddenly, blindingly, seen all the advantages of a union between

Thomas and Clarissa and they do not hesitate to promote the match. They are beginning to regret their open-ended invitation to Thomas to come and mourn with them and can now see a way of killing two birds with one stone. Not that they are heartless or unfeeling, they assure each other – no, certainly not – but darling Clarissa is, let's be honest, the *tiniest* bit of a drag. She is forever dropping in or phoning up and droning on about her biological clock and the misery of living alone and then there is all the fag of having to find a spare man for dinner parties and so forth – getting *really* difficult these days. ('Oh, honestly, darling, not that helpless female from Fulham again.') As for dear old Thomas, well it is the *least* bit dreary having him moping about the place and having to keep up the caring, encouraging thing when you wanted to be getting pissed with that fun couple who have moved in opposite. After all, Claerwen was a sweetie, an absolute poppet – when she wasn't feeling exhausted or had those ghastly pains – but to be perfectly frank he is probably better off without her. There is no reason, no reason at all, why darling Clarissa shouldn't make a perfectly *splendid* mother to dear little Megan and a *wonderful* wife for dear old Thomas . . .

When Clarissa first sees the house she gasps with delight. She stares at the half-timbering, the Tudor chimney pots, the original small rosy red brick tiles, the mullioned windows and the great oak door, and she sighs with deep unalloyed pleasure.

'Oh, Thomas,' she says, misty-eyed. 'It's absolutely magic.'

Thomas beams at her with gratitude. Claerwen had always been anxious about rotting timbers, rising damp, mice in the attics and the trees being so close to the house.

'It's a funny old place,' he says, with a nonchalance

which barely hides his pride. He is very taken with Clarissa, although he feels a little ashamed of his feelings, so soon after Claerwen's death.

'Honestly.' Clarissa is lost in admiration as she stares raptly at the house – she has made him stop the car (a *very* nice old Bentley) at the end of the drive – and she stretches out a hand to him which falls onto his thigh, well, very nearly onto his crotch, and he gives a muffled little gasp which she pretends to ignore. They both stare straight ahead, Clarissa still in her rapt state, until she gives a huge sigh, removes her hand and turns to look at him with innocent sweetness. He swallows and sets the car in motion, hot with sensations he has almost forgotten. Claerwen was far too delicate in the latter years for any of that kind of nonsense.

Clarissa is aware that Thomas will need a certain amount of encouragement in order to overcome his natural reticence with women, especially whilst he is in mourning, but her own feelings are so strong that she finds it impossible to restrain herself and allow their friendship to develop slowly. He has appeared in her life when she is feeling lonely and unloved and she is afraid that he might disappear again before she can win him. She is friendly but charmingly diffident with the two aged biddies who are waiting for her in the drawing-room. She takes in their tweeds (old but good, rather like the Bentley), the hand-knitted jerseys and brogues, and sees two fluffy old dears who seem very ready to be friendly. She enthuses about the house and they watch her, bright eyed and expectant. After luncheon (she thinks it wonderful that they still call it 'luncheon') they show her over the house. She is hardly aware of their intensity as they wait for her reaction. She speaks of atmosphere and declares that it must be haunted but only, she adds hastily, in a happy, delightful way. Olwen and Gwyneth smile mysteriously and exchange a glance. Everything goes swimmingly.

Megan is away at school and, after a tactful period of time and quite a few meetings in London, it is arranged that Thomas will take Clarissa to meet her during the next exeat. They both know they must go slowly here. Megan has been devoted to her sickly mother and will not be looking for a substitute. Megan, however, takes her father's 'friend' at face value and is open and natural. Clarissa is charmed by her. Step-motherhood, she can see, will be a doddle. Nevertheless she is beginning to realise that to be too eager, too pushing, will upset Thomas's fastidious, old-fashioned idea of how ladies behave. She returns to Fulham to wait for Thomas, who has now returned to the Welsh marches, to telephone to arrange another meeting. It is rather too premature to give in her notice at the bank, anyway she is glad to have something to do, but all she can think of is Thomas and the little Tudor manor in the oak woodlands.

Thomas is rather overwhelmed by his reawakened physical passion. The delicate, frail Claerwen raised all his chivalrous, protective instincts but, although he was occasionally disappointed at her lack of interest in the grosser manifestations of his love, she never rejected him. As a young husband Thomas would have preferred a rather more active response but, after her miscarriages, Claerwen became even less responsive and Thomas schooled himself to celibacy. This has not been so difficult as it might have been for many other more lusty men. He is by nature retiring and living as he does, isolated and absorbed with the running of his estate, he has not been distracted by temptation; until now.

Now there is Clarissa. He thinks about her as he goes about his daily business, trying to sort out his feelings. She is so touchingly natural, he thinks, so artlessly affectionate, rather like a trusting child. It is clear – Thomas tells himself – that she has no idea how easily a lonely man might be aroused by her delightfully innocent little ways. After all she has never been married (Clarissa has told him the moving, and entirely fictitious, story of a dear, dead love) and he sees that she is quite inexperienced in the art of flirting.

His friends, knowing him as they do, have been anxious to stress the inexperienced angle. They agree that Clarissa is simply an unspoiled child who has been faithful to her one true – dead – love. Thomas – raised in the remote fastness of the Welsh marches, at thirteen sent away to Shrewsbury School, at nineteen brought home to learn estate management – is easy prey to their assurances. By the time he is twenty-two he is married to Claerwen, at twenty-seven he is a father and now, in his early forties, he is a widower.

So Thomas walks his diminished estate and talks with his few remaining tenants – and thinks about Clarissa and whether she will consider him heartless and shallow if he proposes to her so soon after Claerwen's death. Clarissa, after all, has been so faithful to her dear, dead love.

In her basement flat Clarissa wonders if she were wise to go on about the dear, dead love quite so dramatically. Also she has forgotten what name she has given – on this occasion – to this paragon who has claimed her heart until now; Henry, was it? Or David? Thomas, she feels sure, will remember everything she told him during that touching little scene and Clarissa frowns as she stares out into the damp, dreary yard with its collection of dustbins and debris. She has been careless, very careless. She remembers the first, vital rule, which her really, *really* best friend Georgy has been attempting to instil into Clarissa's head since those early days at school together: 'A good liar must have a good memory.'

Perhaps she need not mention him again? There have been so many variations on this theme over the years, each one tailored to fit the present company, that it is difficult to remember clearly. Despite the fact that it is now perfectly right, enviable even, for a woman to have a career and independence, there is still a tendency for young single women to feel the need to explain the reason for their spinsterhood. It is necessary for them to make it clear that it is by *choice* that they live in dismal basement flats and spend the weekends alone watching videos. The dear, dead love has come in very handy, saving her from humiliation and explanations regarding her continuing single state.

Clarissa, who is neither ambitious nor independent, suspects that she has been a little too eager, too transparent, with boyfriends in the past and she is determined not to make the same mistake with Thomas. She is sure that she is in love with him, although she admits to herself that the house is a tremendous bonus. As she stands at the window – the flat isn't roomy enough for pacing – the vision of the house is forever before her as though indelibly printed on her retina. Despite its charm, however, the house is not chocolate-boxy. It rises from the earth, sturdy as a fortress, functional, sheltering. Already Clarissa can see herself showing it to her friends, down for the weekend from London. She imagines their envy and feels a surge of joyful anticipation. She clenches her fists in an agony of impatience but knows that she will wait for as long as it takes. Once again the vision of the house superimposes itself on the dustbins.

'I want it,' she mutters childishly, setting her jaw. 'I *want* it.'

When Thomas telephones it is almost impossible to hide her frustration but she schools herself to sound cool, gently asking how he is coping, enquiring after Megan, after the aunts. She makes these enquiries sound no more than the interest shown by a caring acquaintance and she senses his faint anxiety at the other end of the line. When he invites her to stay for the weekend she gives a well-judged coo of pleasure, tempered with the suggestion that he is being far too kind and that he mustn't feel the least bit obliged to entertain her. The words *'whilst you are still grieving'* hang in the air and Thomas, who has barely given Claerwen a thought in the last few weeks, hastens to assure Clarissa that her company will be just what he needs. She allows herself to be persuaded and, with a sense of victory and enormous relief, she replaces the telephone receiver and punches the air with her clenched fists. Georgy would be proud of her.

Thomas stands by the telephone looking fatuously pleased with himself. Aunt Olwen, passing through the hall, beams at him and he beams back at her. They stand so, beaming back and forth, until he pulls himself together and tells her the glad tidings.

Aunt Olwen, who has listened to his side of the entire conversation from behind the morning-room door, pats him gently on the shoulder. 'Such a nice girl,' she says encouragingly (she pronounces it 'gel'). 'It's good for you to have some younger company, my dear boy.'

She has already sensed Clarissa's desire for the house and sees how it might be used to good advantage. She and Gwyneth are getting old and they must find another custodian to whom they can bequeath the house and its secrets. By rights it should be Megan. She is, after all, a Mortimer; a descendant of the great Marcher Lord who was hanged as a traitor on a dark November day more than six hundred years ago, accused of seducing a lonely, ambitious queen and murdering a weak, vain king. He forfeited his immortal soul for earthly power and glory, yet many considered him a great patriot and, since no attainder was ever passed, the Mortimers kept their huge inheritance and his Irish wife her estates. His grandson acquitted himself well at Crecy and the Earldom of March was restored to him. The castles and towers have long since crumbled but a Mortimer built this house in the reign of Henry Tudor and there have been Mortimers here ever since.

Yet Olwen and Gwyneth are not convinced that Megan has the right qualities for guardianship, even though she has the Sight. She is her mother's daughter: kind, gentle, God-fearing, and lately she has expressed the desire to become a nun. Thomas is not too old to have more children and Clarissa looks a likely candidate for bearing Mortimers better equipped for the task. Olwen continues to smile as she climbs the stairs to find Gwyneth, to tell her that Clarissa will be coming for the weekend.

2

Other buildings have stood on this site in the oak woods: several stone cottages have fallen into disrepair and, before that, a mud hut or two. Behind the house, deep in the wood are the standing stones. They lean a little, grey and pitted, rough to the touch, forming a circle. Before the stones were raised, the Goddess was worshipped in the sacred grove; the earth is soaked with human blood and bones rot beneath the cool green grass. Long before Christianity arrived on these shores, the Druids believed in the immortality of the human soul. The Romans ruthlessly hunted down and attempted to destroy this cult but the Druids continued to meet secretly wherever they found the Goddess, in stone or tree or cave, and there they made their offering. Here, in the oak grove, beyond the circle of the standing stones, hidden by the house, strange things still happen. No gardener has ever been allowed into the grove or the woods behind the house.

Even Thomas half believes the old legend that the fortunes of his house are bound up in the great trees. If they fall, then his family will perish. He laughs about it but it is he who makes sure that the wood is kept free of disease and weakness. The trees are strong and tall and healthy, their roots digging deep, drinking in the dark, rich nourishment buried below. It is, however, the women of the family who know that it is the Goddess who protects them. It is She who must be worshipped and appeased.

Thomas's grandfather marries his cousin, so that she becomes doubly Mortimer, by birth and by marriage. She is a strange, fierce woman with grey eyes that flicker and shine, like bright light striking cold sea water; Mortimer eyes. She sees the storm clouds that gather in the hills, the lightning that flashes on the mountain tops, and knows that on such nights as these the old spells live again and magic is abroad, riding the wind. Her son is a gentle man, loving the land, content with his lot, but her daughters worship with her in the grove and learn to sacrifice to the Goddess. When she dies, Gwyneth and Olwen watch through the night by their mother's open coffin and, in the early hours, they rise up and take her body in its shroud and carry it into the grove. At her own wish they bury her deep in the damp black earth beneath the trees. The grave is ready prepared and cold white moonlight pours down between the branches as they commit her body to the ground. The coffin is filled with carefully wrapped stones and fixed down by their mother's Welsh manservant, ready for the undertakers to carry to the little churchyard on the bare, windy hill. Thomas's mother also lies there, in the grove, eased out of pain and suffering by her sisters-in-law's knowledge of herb lore. More stones were carried to the churchyard but Gwyneth and Olwen know that the souls of their mother and sister-in-law walk free in the grove beneath the great trees, amongst the standing stones.

But who will bury Gwyneth and Olwen in the grove when the time comes? Who will protect the grove, worship the Goddess and tend the unmarked graves? It is vital that the house is passed from their custodianship to the right guardian. When it becomes clear that poor Claerwen will bear no more children it seems kind to help her out of her life. It is quite simple. Both Gwyneth and Olwen know that half the battle is in the mind. When someone loses the will to live the rest is easy. Darling Claerwen barely struggled against their whispers which drifted gently but inexorably into her ears as she lay, weak and helpless, on her bed.

Now they watch and wait. Will Clarissa be the vehicle for the next custodian? They have discounted Megan. There is something missing, some necessary inherited knowledge. When they encourage her into the cool, dim grove she shivers and starts, staring about anxiously. She hears the echoes of past deeds, the screams and sobs of the victims; she feels a cold current of air brushing her bare arms and her heart is filled with sadness.

'I don't like it here,' she says and the aunts rustle restlessly and sigh impatiently. At her age they were already sacrificing to the Goddess, willing, eager little pupils of their mother's art.

'Stay a little longer,' they wheedle. 'Don't go yet. Feel the stones. How warm they are. Come. Touch them. Kneel just here on the soft grass . . .'

But she evades their insistent hands and runs back into the sunny garden and they cluck their teeth and shake their heads over her foolishness. Of course, they tell each other, she might be a late starter, it might come in time – but the years pass and it becomes clear that Megan will never become the Goddess's servant. Now they feel that they must take precautionary steps, delighted that Thomas has acted so promptly. They wonder if Clarissa is genuinely aware that the house is haunted; small beer compared to the magic in the grove but it would be a splendid start. Of course, it is the Mortimer blood which will carry the necessary knowledge but some help on Clarissa's side will do no harm. They are eager to see her again.

Their eagerness is nothing compared to Clarissa's. She is breathless with it. She is determined to encourage Thomas into a proposal if she can do so and she counts the hours to the weekend. She reviews the urban contents of her wardrobe and goes out to buy some clothes which will be more suitable for the country, though not so suitable as to be frumpish. She smiles benignly to herself as she remembers the two old biddies in their tweeds and home-knit jerseys, convinced that they are on her side. Clarissa hums happily to herself as she unpacks her goodies and lays the lovely new clothes out on her bed, imagining herself as Thomas's wife, mother of his children, the lady of the manor. Maybe she'll become a Sloane Ranger and go with Megan to the pony club. She wonders if it would be jumping the gun to buy a Barbour and a pair of green Hunter wellies but decides against it. Apart from anything else, her Barclaycard can't stand up to any more extravagance at the moment. For the hundredth time she glances at her watch. This time tomorrow she will be there.

Thomas, too, is excited. He is surprised at himself. It is unlike him to be so unrestrained. He tries to remember how he felt when he first fell in love with Claerwen whom he knew from childhood upwards. She was so gentle and shy and his feelings were always of a protective kind. Even in his youth he never felt so virile and manly as he does now, whilst he waits for Clarissa. Thomas reminds himself that he is only forty-two and probably in his prime. Then, too, Clarissa is such a lively, feminine woman that it is hardly surprising that he should feel so, well, randy is the word that leaps unbidden to his mind. Faintly embarrassed at his thoughts, he straightens his shoulders and pulls in his stomach, staring at himself in the long looking-glass in his dressing-room. His critical eye notices the thickening waistline and greying hair and he feels dismayed. Perhaps it is rather presumptuous to ask a young woman to take on a middle-aged widower and his child, not to mention two ageing aunts.

His friends have told him how popular Clarissa is, how much in demand she is socially, what a terrific friend she is. He already knows about her loyalty to the dear, dead love. Doubt – deadly, confidence-sapping – creeps in round his heart. He has been a fool to think he might stand a chance with such a warm, charming woman. He remembers her voice on the telephone, cool and friendly but no more; her faint surprise when he suggested she should visit him again. No doubt she found him a bore, was simply being kind to this dull, middle-aged widower, sympathising with his grief. Perhaps their mutual friends had warned her. *'Be kind to poor old Thomas, he's in a bad way'* and so on. He cringes at the thought of her pity and decides that he must cancel her visit. He cannot stand the humiliation. His shoulders sag a little as he turns away from the mirror . . . to find Aunt Olwen standing close behind him.

'My God, aunt!' he gasps, clutching his chest. 'You made me jump. I didn't hear you.'

'I'm so sorry, my dear boy. So sorry. Didn't you hear me knock? I thought you said "Come in." Sit down here for a moment.'

She presses him down in a chair and he is briefly aware of her strange grey eyes, a little cloudy with age, now, but still keen and disturbing, looking into his own, probing his thoughts.

He swallows and tries to smile at her. 'Sorry. Miles away. You know how it is.'

She is smiling gently at him, patting his shoulder. 'Aunt Gwyneth was just saying that you should come down for a drink before dinner. We're feeling rather jolly at the thought of our visitor arriving tomorrow. I'm sure Clarissa is excited, too. She rather loved our dear old house, didn't she?'

Her fingers grip his shoulder, her eyes still stare into his, and he feels a measure of strength returning: of courage flowing back through his veins. Clarissa *did* like the house. He remembers her cry of delight, her hand on his thigh and other little gestures of affection, and his manhood re-asserts itself. Not only did she like the house, she liked *him*, Thomas Mortimer, middle-aged widower or not. It was perfectly clear. Now, suddenly, he can remember all sorts of reassuring signs . . .

He takes a deep breath and realises that Aunt Olwen is still bending over him, watching him. He gives himself a little shake and chuckles somewhat shamefacedly. He feels he's been in a bit of trance, away with the fairies, and wonders what she must think of him. Dear old thing to worry about him . . .

'I'm fine, aunt,' he says confidently. 'Don't know what came over me. Bless you. I should like a drink.'

'Good, good,' she says, straightening up. 'You're looking well, dear boy. Aunt Gwyneth and I were remarking on it earlier. A fine upstanding figure of a man. Never looked better.'

Thomas beams at her as he rises to his feet and steals another look at himself in the glass. Now that the scales have dropped from his eyes he can see that he *is* looking well, fit and strong; the grey hair at his temples lends a touch of distinction and he looks healthy and tanned. He smirks a little, flexing his muscles . . . and remembers Claerwen.

Olwen pauses by the door, looking back. 'Another thing, my dear boy,' she says gently. 'You can't grieve forever. And darling Claerwen wouldn't have wanted it. You have Megan to think of, remember. Claerwen wouldn't have wanted this to become a house of mourning. We never forget our dead, they are always with us, but the quick, those of us who are still living, must give thought for the future.'

'"*The quick and the dead,*"' murmurs Thomas, wondering where he has heard the words before.

'Come along.' His aunt's voice is oddly sharp. 'Stop dreaming. Aunt Gwyneth must be wondering where we've got to.'

Thomas sneaks one last admiring glance in the looking-glass and follows her downstairs.

In her little flat, Clarissa is writing a letter to her very best friend, Georgy. Since school they have shared nearly everything. They did a drama course together, applied for similar jobs, lived together in a flat in Hammersmith, but now Georgy has gone to America – a once-in-a-lifetime offer of a job in an advertising agency in New York, found through a friend of a friend – and Clarissa is left to struggle alone. It is Georgy who has been the one with the energy and the ideas, the one who has stimulated the idle, indecisive Clarissa, been the force in her life. How pleased, then, Georgy will be to see that her lazy old chum can pull off such an amazing feat.

It will show her, thinks Clarissa, busily scribbling a glowing description of Thomas and the house, that she's not the only one with get-up-and-go.

She goes on to describe the aunts and explains how nervous she is about the coming weekend. How she wishes Georgy were here, to wish her luck, bolster her confidence, give her advice. Yet a small part of her feels a smug satisfaction that she has done so well without her really, *really* best friend. This will teach Georgy to mock her about her inability to take a decision or achieve anything worthwhile. Smiling to herself, Clarissa seals the envelope, grabs her coat and purse and hurries out to the post office. She can't wait for Georgy to have the good tidings.

3

The weekend is a great success: everyone is on their best behaviour. The aunts, outwardly fluffy and sweet, are watching Clarissa closely. Once again they are aware of her desire for the house and they make quite certain that she sees it to its maximum advantage. It is swept and garnished for her and she exclaims with rapture as each new treasure is revealed. When she cries, 'Oh, it's a house to *die* for,' the aunts, unfamiliar with modern-speak, nod approvingly. She might have to do just that. No sacrifice is too great for the house – or for the Goddess. Clarissa's attitude delights them and, by the end of the weekend, they are confident that she has been sent to them expressly for their purpose.

Thomas feels much the same. Clarissa continues to charm him and makes him aware of his loneliness. How pleasant it would be to have her here sharing his life, he thinks – and wonders how soon he can propose. Quite properly he feels that he must first speak to the aunts and to Megan. The aunts encourage him without reservation. They manage to imply, without any disrespect to Claerwen, that he deserves a lively, cheerful companion and that they will all feel the benefit of Clarissa's presence. He is grateful for their approval but refuses to make the final move until he has spoken with Megan. She will be home for half-term in a few days' time and he thinks it is only right that he should discuss the prospect of a step-mother with her.

The aunts chafe a little at such sensibility. In their youth, children were not given such consideration but they do not wish to antagonise Thomas so they continue to smile and nod agreeably – and wait impatiently for Megan's homecoming.

Megan is unprepared for the news. Other girls might have guessed something is afoot but not Megan. Thomas hopes that she has suspected that Clarissa is more than just a friend – surely bringing her to tea on the exeat was significant? – but his daughter is unaware of anything out of the ordinary and Thomas has to flounder awkwardly. Despite his aunts' assurances, he still feels guilty that he has been able to forget darling Claerwen quite so readily. He is ashamed that he is so eager to replace her. During the long drive from the station, he tries to explain to the puzzled Megan just how he feels. He becomes confused and repeats himself and, quite unreasonably, almost resents Megan's surprise and her inability to help him out of this difficult scene.

Sitting beside him, slender and pale in the unbecoming school uniform, she looks exactly like her mother and an equal blend of love and guilt makes him irritable.

'It's you that I'm thinking of,' he cries, with a quite staggering disregard for the truth. 'A girl of your age needs a mother. I'm no use to you and the aunts are too old.' He glances at her quickly and descends to common emotional blackmail. 'And of course I'm lonely, too, without darling Mummie, now, and you away at school.'

His voice is plaintive and trembles a little with genuine self-pity. It *is* hard that he is so lonely, with no-one to care for him. God knows, he's had little enough attention over the last few years with Claerwen always ill. Surely it's not too much to ask that he has some pleasure out of life?

Megan watches him thoughtfully. Responsive to many things that are usually beyond earthly awareness she is often slow to understand her fellow creatures. As she grows older she senses her aunts' influence and power, although it is outside her comprehension. She only knows that she must avoid it, yet she is not afraid. There is some barrier between them and herself which protects her and she is content to move within her own world where there is peace and light and silence. It is only when the outside world collides with this other world that she becomes nervous and ill-at-ease. Now, she realises, is one of those moments. She concentrates on all that her father has been saying and sees that she has been stupid.

'Do you want to marry Clarissa?' she asks. 'Well, I don't mind. Why should I?'

Her father turns to stare at her in amazement, causing the car to swerve violently. A passing motorist gestures rudely and screams insults whilst his passengers stare reprovingly and smugly from the back seat as Thomas pulls into the verge and wipes his brow. He feels as if some huge weight has been lifted from his heart.

'Of course I don't mind.' She smiles at him reassuringly. 'I'm sorry I was so slow.'

'No, no,' he says hastily. 'Not slow. Why should you . . . ? How could you have . . . ?' Her generosity makes him want to reward her in some way. 'It's not that I don't love Mummie or . . . or anything . . .'

Megan is silent. His remark is superfluous. To Megan life and death are indivisible, two sides of the same thing. Claerwen can never be closer to them than she is now. Why should he stop loving her? This love has nothing to do with Clarissa. Megan perceives that this is another area where the two worlds might collide and she opts for safety.

'Of course not. I know that. I liked Clarissa. Is she at home now?'

'No,' says Thomas, setting the car in motion. She might have been if he'd only known how readily Megan would accept the situation. 'No, she isn't. But I hope you'll meet her again soon. Oh, darling, bless you for being so understanding.'

Megan smiles because he is happy and settles herself back in her seat. She waits for the first sight of the house with the usual mixed feelings. She loves it but feels the danger. She knows now that her father, who is a Mortimer, cannot see the shades of his ancestors. Yet her mother, who had the Sight, was aware of their presence. The aunts are different again. Their allegiance is to something old and terrible and cruel and Megan fears for them.

They are waiting for her, coming to kiss her cheek, to pat her shoulder and take her overnight case.

'A special tea,' they murmur, herding her into the drawing-room. 'Your favourite cake. You'd like that? You would? Splendid. So how was your journey? How is school this term?'

Over her head they question Thomas with their eyes and he nods back, grinning foolishly, shrugging and gesturing to show how needless were their fears, how delightfully generous his daughter has been. Their relief manifests itself in a rush of affection towards Megan and all is sweetness and light. It only remains now for Thomas to propose to Clarissa.

He does it on the lawn before the house so as to remind her of all that is wrapped up in the proposal. Even now he cannot quite believe that she will accept. She can see the sweep of the gravel drive and the steps leading up to the paved terrace. The sun shines on warm mellowed brick and twinkles on the glass panes of the mullioned windows. Tall oaks line the drive to the left and march round to the back of the house to join the wood, but away to the right the lawn drops gently to the river. Beyond the river the small neat fields rise to the rocky knees of the mountains whose stark outlines are clear cut and majestic against the chalky blue of the sky. It is a magic day. The magic is in the air and all about them as they pace across the turf. The aunts, in their rooms on the first floor, watch them. They concentrate their minds and their wills upon the couple so that Clarissa believes that she has entered into some fairyland where nothing is quite real. She feels light and strong; capable of anything.

Thomas is slightly less receptive to their power but he feels his confidence growing as Clarissa turns to smile at him. He swallows, seizes her hand and starts to speak. He is quite eloquent – for Thomas – and utters the well-worn phrases with all the fervour of a man who has just invented them. Clarissa is so moved that her answer is quick and very positive. She tells him that she, too, has loved him from the very first moment they met and that the dear, dead love – David? John? Sensibly she avoids naming him – has for the first time been superseded by these new, uncontrollable feelings. This is clever of Clarissa for it enables Thomas to explain that this is exactly how *he* feels about poor darling Claerwen and thus does away with any tiresome feelings of remorse. With a few well-chosen – and carefully rehearsed – words she implies that their special love is above the more humdrum affection of your average couple. It is a gift from the gods and it is their duty to accept it whole-heartedly.

As she smiles mistily up at him – she has remembered to wear flat heels since Thomas is only just above average height and she is a tall girl – he can barely contain his joy. He wants to beat his chest and howl like a dog. Instead he takes her outstretched hands and bends to kiss her raised lips.

The aunts sigh with relief, switch off the special effects and hurry downstairs to be at hand for the announcement and the champagne.

*   *   *

Clarissa returns to London so as to hand in her notice at the bank and to her landlord. She can hardly believe her good fortune. She has taken some photographs of Thomas, strategically placed so that every aspect of the front of the house is also shown, and when these are developed she totes them round to all her girlfriends. Some are silent, some are gushing, some are spiteful, all are envious. Clarissa is expansive with self-satisfaction.

'You must come down,' she says. 'Come and stay. There's plenty of room. At least ten bedrooms. Oh and just *here*, out of sight, is the river and just beyond are the mountains. There are three or four farms on the estate and the most marvellous woods. Lovely, lovely walks and all on one's own land. No, I'm not a bit worried about Megan. She's a poppet. We get on ter*rif*ically well. And she's away at school most of the time, of course. The aunts? Heavens, no! Not the *least* bit stuffy. Really jolly old dears. They've welcomed me with open arms. To be honest, the first wife was a bit of a wet blanket, you know, semi-invalid and so on, and they really are such *fun*. You should have seen them when Thomas opened the champagne after he'd proposed. He'd put it on ice, just hoping. Isn't it too sweet? Look, here's one taken from the end of the drive. Yes, it is a long one, isn't it? What? Oh, that's Thomas's car. Yes I believe it *is* a Bentley. You know me. Hopeless about cars. Very old, apparently. Vintage, or something. Oh, he's *such* a darling. He was at Shrewsbury with Charlie Radcliffe. You must know the Radcliffes. I was at school with Caroline's little sister. Oh, darling, don't tease. Of *course* Thomas isn't a Lord . . .'

'How did she do it?' the friends ask each other between gritted teeth. 'Why *her*? Why didn't Caroline invite *us* to meet this bloody wonderful Thomas? Oh, it would be Clarissa of all people.'

Radiant with triumph and happiness, Clarissa winds up her London life and prepares for the country. She longs to ask all her friends to a really splendid wedding but knows that it is too soon after Claerwen's death. Thomas would be shocked at such a suggestion. No, she must be content with a quiet, local, civil ceremony. Then she will invite all her chums to stay in turn. She is sorry that her one really, *really* best friend, dearest Georgy, cannot be with her but she will send her all the details and masses of photographs. So far Georgy has been slightly less enthusiastic than could be expected . . . Clarissa wishes that her mother were still alive to witness her daughter's cleverness. After a few years of marriage her father escaped, disappearing into one of the Dominions and never heard of since, and there are no siblings to rejoice with her. Her mother's advice, Clarissa knows, would have been simple and to the point. 'Go for it!' she would have told her daughter – and Clarissa has every intention of doing just that.

She wonders what Thomas's friends will think of his behaviour. They might all react as the Radcliffes have but there is a faint chance that some nosey, interfering well-wisher might advise him to wait a little. She longs to be with Thomas and all the time she is apart from him she fears that some trick of fate might dash the cup of happiness from her lips before she has barely sipped it. Thomas has suggested that they wait until Megan breaks up for the summer holidays – another four long weeks away – so that she can be at the ceremony and, as the days pass, Clarissa becomes more nervous. Sitting alone in her flat, she begins to wonder if such good fortune can truly be hers. It is so rare to meet a man who is happy to marry a woman who has no desire to be anything but a contented wife and mother. This is what Clarissa has longed for ever since she left school but the pressure of her peers has never allowed her to admit it. She does not want to wear sharp little suits and carry a lap-top or a mobile telephone. To be honest, she is not *exactly* delighted at the thought of cooking – she can manage pasta and boils a mean egg but serious cooking is beyond her and she relies heavily on take-aways – nevertheless she has seen enough to know that the aunts are in control and she has no intention of attempting to usurp their positions. She is confident that she can make Thomas happy but terrified lest he should change his mind about her, and as her fear increases, an idea creeps into her mind . . .

One early morning she telephones Thomas for a chat. He hears some little tremor in the voice, the occasional sigh, the lack of laughter, and he demands to know what is wrong. After a great deal of hesitation on her part and cajoling on Thomas's she tells him that the landlord is being difficult. He wants the flat for a friend of his and she must either sign a new lease or move out. What is more – here her voice drops a little and a fearful note creeps in – he is paying . . . she hesitates . . . well, how can she put it, unwelcome attentions to her, coming round late at night and making – a longer pause here – well, suggestions.

Thomas's protective instincts, always so strong and reliable, surge forward. Until now he has seen Clarissa as sexy, amusing, confident, brave. Now he imagines her cowering in her little room; weak and frightened. 'You must come at once!' he cries. 'Damn the man. I'll come and deal with him and bring you home. I'll come now. Don't answer the door until I come.'

'Oh, darling,' she says tremulously, her brain working quickly – it would be a pity if he ran into the owner of the flat who is a dear little lady who lives upstairs – 'may I really come? Are you sure? What would the aunts think? You know? Us not being married yet. Would they think it a bit off? Perhaps I could go to friends . . .'

'You'll do nothing of the sort,' he bellows masterfully. 'You'll come here where you belong. I don't give a damn what anyone thinks. I'll make a few phone calls and get right off.'

'No, wait a moment, darling. Listen. I could catch the train. There's one at twelve-thirty-five to Bristol – I really don't want to stay here any longer than I can help . . .'

'Absolutely,' he shouts. 'Quite right. Leave your things and come. We'll deal with all that later. I'll drive to Bristol to meet you.'

Delighted with his reaction, though slightly ashamed at her deviousness, Clarissa sheds a few tears of relief and hastens to finish her packing, the words *here where you belong* ringing happily in her ears. Before she leaves she makes careful arrangements to have her boxes sent after her. She has no intention of allowing Thomas to bump into darling Mrs Johnson who has always been so obliging about late rent and other minor problems. When everything else is quite ready she gives her key to Mrs Johnson with instructions about her belongings, hugs her warmly and climbs into the taxi.

'Paddington Station,' she tells the driver and falls back onto the seat quite exhausted.

4

Once the honeymoon is over, Clarissa adjusts swiftly to her new life. Not that the honeymoon is in any way world-shatteringly exciting. The wedding is brought forward so that reputations are not at risk but Thomas cannot afford to spend too much time away from the estate in June. The newly-weds go to a small country hotel in the mountains for a few days but, when they return, it is the aunts who look as if they have had the holiday. They are pink cheeked, bright eyed and full of energy and Clarissa laughingly suggests that they've been celebrating the longest day, a secret midsummer solstice all on their own.

She is quite happy with her short holiday. She does not crave Thomas's constant company – she has discovered that a little of it goes rather a long way – and, besides, she wants to settle down to the local round. She wishes to become a fully-paid-up Sloane Ranger and wonders where to begin. The Barbour has been purchased along with a very nice corduroy skirt and a pair of very fetching knickerbockers. Clarissa knows that shoes are vital and, since her bank account is unable to rise to Guccis, she has been on a successful little foray to Russell and Bromley. The contents of her wardrobe are now ready to be worn in the great game known as Country Life, even the crucial pearls are at the ready – but there is a distinct absence of players.

Thomas seems to have no friends and the aunts don't entertain. Clarissa waits hopefully for a few weeks and then hints that he might like to invite a few chums round for supper.

He stares at her blankly. 'Chums?' he repeats, looking a little puzzled.

Clarissa feels a faint, very faint, twinge of irritation. She smiles brightly at him. 'Yes,' she says. 'Chums. Friends. Neighbours. Mates. People one knows. What do you call them round here?'

He laughs at her ready wit and shakes his head, still chuckling. 'To tell you the truth,' he tells her, 'we don't bother to entertain any more. Poor Claerwen was never really up to it and the aunts are too old. Oh dear. Is that going to be a problem? Are you missing your London friends?'

He doesn't add the word 'already' but it is implicit in his tone which is the tiniest bit reproachful.

Clarissa is quick to see the danger and slips an arm through his. 'Of course not,' she says, laughing in her turn at such a ridiculous notion. 'How could I when I have you and the aunts and all this lovely countryside? No, it's just that I didn't want to seem backward in meeting your friends. I wouldn't want to seem rude or unfriendly. I know what it can be like in the country.'

He pats her arm reassuringly. 'Don't worry about that,' he says. 'We're very remote here, you know. There're no young people round here at all, as far as I know.'

'Is that so?' she asks, her spirits sinking. 'What *none*?'

'I expect there are in the village,' he says thoughtfully. 'Locals and so on. It's not fashionable country, you know, and it isn't commuter land. I'm afraid you'll just have to put up with me, my darling.'

He laughs heartily and she joins in, although her laughter has a faintly hollow note.

'Poor old Megan,' she says lightly. 'She must find the holidays a bit dull.'

Thomas looks thoughtful again. 'She's a very self-contained child,' he says. 'I think she's glad to get home for some peace and quiet. She finds it hard to be constantly surrounded by people. The lack of privacy at boarding-school tires her. Perhaps it's because she's an only child.'

'Perhaps,' agrees Clarissa, although she – also an only child – has never known this problem. On the contrary, she is outgoing, gregarious and finds her own company very dull. It has been this need for companionship which has driven her friends mad. However, she doesn't despair just yet. She is quite certain that there are other like-minded people out there somewhere and she just needs to be able to locate them. Meanwhile she has the house. It still charms and enthralls her and it's wonderful not to have the drudgery of the office.

The aunts are delighted that Clarissa is so friendly. There is no question of them withdrawing to their own quarters or being tactful about Clarissa being the real chatelaine. She has no desire to take the reins of housekeeping into her idle hands and is quite happy to let things go on just as before. Nan Ellis comes up from the village to do the rough and some of the cooking and Clarissa is allowed to relax and enjoy being Thomas's wife. She drifts about the house, goes for walks and reads. The aunts prepare little treats and delicacies and Clarissa begins to feel like a dearly-loved child. They are always ready to stop for a chat and, as she gets to know them, Clarissa relaxes. The two old dears are just as much fun as some of her friends and much nicer to her. She is determined to be happy and contented and is looking forward to Megan's company when she comes home for the holidays.

It takes only a day or two to see that Megan is going to be no help at all on the social front. She has no desire to do much more than wander in the lanes and hills or read endlessly. Her only other pleasure is taken in going to see the nuns in the convent across the valley. It is clear that the aunts disapprove of this, although they do not openly discuss it even when Clarissa brings up the subject herself.

'Bit worrying,' she says, 'a girl of that age rushing off to be with nuns every spare minute.'

The aunts are silent but their faces are serious, even grim; expressions that Clarissa has not yet seen on those jolly, rosy old faces. Her curiosity is roused and she probes a little further.

'Perhaps we should suggest that Thomas puts his foot down?' she suggests cautiously. Is it rather too early to be airing her opinions? 'It's such an impressionable age, isn't it? We don't want a nun in the family, do we?'

She laughs lightly but is surprised to see a glance which is almost venomous pass between them. They mutter and rustle and pass out of the room but there is a breath of something ancient and ruthless which seems to linger and Clarissa rubs her bare arms and shivers a little. When she mentions the matter to Thomas he frowns a little and shakes his head.

'We have to face it,' he says at last. 'Megan comes from a family that has always had its share of *religieuses*. I think Claerwen regretted not entering the convent. It was in her mind for a long time before she married me.'

Clarissa is shocked. She hasn't realised that women still become nuns. Surely it's all quite outdated? 'But you can't want Megan to become a *nun*!' she says, amazed. 'For heaven's sake! It's positively Gothic.'

'It's a question of a vocation,' answers Thomas firmly. 'I wouldn't want to stand in her way if she has a true vocation.'

Clarissa stares at him, appalled. She remembers his ancient lineage and how cut off he is here in the wilds and wonders if he has actually caught up with the twentieth century at all. Some of his ideas are extremely antiquated, no doubt about that, but really . . . a *nun*!

'Honestly,' she says unwisely. 'It's really bizarre. Anyway, the aunts don't approve.'

He looks at her coolly. 'It's none of their business,' he says. 'Megan is my child. Her mother might have been happier in a convent and I think Megan is very like her.'

Clarissa, misjudging his mood, makes some tactless remarks about Claerwen and Thomas reacts rather sharply. They quarrel and Thomas becomes angry. He looks quite formidable and, seeing that she has gone too far, she backs off a little. It is too late. A coolness has arisen between them. Thomas is quiet and withdrawn; he says that he is feeling restless and that it will be better if he sleeps in his dressing-room so as not to disturb her. Clarissa is hurt, he has made her feel like an outsider and she loses her confidence. Thomas's darker moods are not easy to handle and she does not quite know how to make overtures of peace.

The aunts notice the rift in the lute and take measures to restore harmony. They draw Clarissa back more closely into their activities, leaving Megan free to wander, and Clarissa begins to relax and to enjoy herself again. The three of them spend hours over morning coffee and afternoon tea, not to mention drinks before dinner. Clarissa can see that these two old darlings have got the good old Sloane code of What Really Matters well in hand. The drinks are delicious, especially the ones that the aunts have concocted themselves.

'Nothing but natural ingredients,' they assure her, the first time they suggest an alternative to her usual gin and tonic. 'Elderberry, sloe . . .' their voices murmur indistinguishably as they hand her the brimming glass.

She sips cautiously . . . raises her eyebrows and takes a good glop. 'Hey,' she says, 'this is really, *really* good.'

They nod, bright eyed, smiling encouragingly, raising their own glasses to her. Later, after dinner, she feels warm and happy and sexy and she seeks out Thomas who is watching the television in the small, panelled book-room. She sits beside him, snuggling against him, her hand on his thigh. He is ready to be coaxed and he puts an arm about her, easily distracted from the late evening news. He has missed their intimacy but has felt that it is up to her to make the first move to thaw the frostiness which chills the atmosphere between them.

'Darling!' he says, amused but faintly shocked at a rather daringly explicit embrace. 'Honestly. Not here.'

'You're no fun any more,' she slurs, pressing closer. 'Where then?'

Thomas is delighted to have the old Clarissa pressing close to him; he is flattered by this unbridled desire for his body and, glad to be back in tune together, they disappear upstairs.

From the shadowy hall, the aunts watch approvingly. They nod and smile at each other and slip quietly away.

'Can you see them?' whispers Megan. 'Can you sense them all about you? The house feels so crowded sometimes, have you noticed?'

Clarissa, drowsing over a book in the small saloon during the long hours between tea and dinner, starts awake. 'What? What is it? Noticed what?' She stares about her.

'The Silent Ones,' breathes Megan's voice in her ear. 'So many of them. I can't always see them clearly but I can feel them. Can you?'

Clarissa feels the hair rising on the back of her neck as her eyes attempt to pierce the gloom of the darkening room.

'The Little One is standing by your knee,' murmurs Megan. 'See how small his shape is? He died in agony of diphtheria. These are the shades of my ancestors who have been taken unwillingly out of life.'

Clarissa presses herself back into the chair, swallowing a little.

'The nuns say that their souls are with God,' says Megan dreamily, 'and that these are simply echoes of their earthly forms. Probably because their ends were violent or sad the echoes remain earthbound. See – over there? There is the shade of a young girl who hanged herself from a beam in the dairy. She had a child by her lover, a married man, and they took the child from her and sent him away. She went mad with grief and hanged herself.'

Clarissa pulls herself together, although her heart knocks uncomfortably in her breast. 'I can't see anything,' she begins sharply – but she stares uneasily into the corner. Is that a figure moving in the shadows by the tall bookcase? The curtains billow a little as the wind rises and she gives a tiny scream.

'What is it?' Megan is leaning right forward over the back of the chair and looking at her with some surprise.

'Nothing,' says Clarissa shortly. She bites her lip, cross at her show of weakness. 'Nothing at all. Put the light on, do. I hadn't realised how dark it's getting.'

It is a dark chilly day, more like November than September, and the small, wood-panelled room looks gloomy in the half-light. She looks at Megan, who has switched on the lamp standing on the small table near the chair and is now sitting beside her. For the first time she notices that Megan's eyes are a dark, slatey blue, quite unlike the light grey of the aunts' or Thomas's eyes. There is a pure innocent beauty in the little face and she feels oddly uneasy.

'Wouldn't you like to have a friend to stay?' she asks her abruptly. 'Some company of your own age?'

Megan watches her, puzzled at this suggestion. 'I don't need company,' she says gently. She glances around her.

'There are so many friends already here. Thank you,' she adds politely.

Clarissa realises that she needs a drink, needs one very badly, and she smiles and tries to give a little laugh. 'Oh, well, then,' she says nonchalantly. 'Just a thought.'

It occurs to her that should any of Megan's friends come to stay she might scare them to death. She finds that she is glancing over her shoulder and laughs hysterically.

Megan continues to watch her. 'I didn't mean to frighten you,' she says. 'Only, I thought you were looking at the Little One, you see. It was the angle of your head.'

'Has he gone?' asks Clarissa involuntarily.

Megan finds this as puzzling as her father's reassurance about still loving her mother. The quick and the dead are bound together throughout eternity. Where should the Little One go? She answers what she perceives to be Clarissa's real question. 'He won't hurt you,' she says kindly. 'Perhaps you would like a drink?'

'Yes,' says Clarissa quickly. 'Yes. I would.'

They leave the room together and, in the light, bright drawing-room where the heavy curtains are already drawn against the dusk, Clarissa gulps a great breath of relief. The aunts are there, watching her, sensing that she has experienced something unusual. Is she beginning to respond to the house at last? They move forward, drawing her to the fire, pouring a drink, their voices reassuring, their hands kindly upon her arms.

Megan climbs the stairs feeling the Little One beside her. She goes into her bedroom and leans from the window, listening to the bell for Vespers, its chimes blowing on the wind. Sliding to her knees she opens her prayer book and begins to say the office for the third evening of the month.

5

For some days Clarissa remains shaken at what has happened in the small saloon. She cannot rid herself of the notion that she is being watched and she feels uneasy in the dark passages that lead to the kitchen and the laundry room. Claerwen's ill-health made it necessary for a bathroom and small kitchenette to be built into the rooms adjoining her bedroom and Clarissa is grateful for it. She knows that she would never have the courage, now, to go out into the corridor alone at night. If it had been anyone but Megan she would have put the whole thing down to a childish prank, an attempt to frighten her, but she knows that Megan is utterly sincere. Of course, it could simply be that Megan is potty, a sandwich or two short of a picnic, but in her heart she knows that this is not so. She is afraid to mention it to Thomas lest he feels that she is in some way criticising Megan again, but she is determined to bring a breath of normality back into her own life. She realises that, although the aunts are good fun, she is missing her friends and feels a real need to have a good session with people of her own age. In a week or so Megan will be back at school and she is determined that she will invite a small group of her chums down for the weekend. Perhaps the Radcliffes might like to come, as well as a couple of her girlfriends? She has been reluctant to look too keen lest her friends suspect that she is not perfectly content with her new life but now, three months after her wedding, she feels that she might reasonably extend invitations without raising suspicions.

'I was wondering,' she says to Thomas as he potters between bedroom and dressing-room, 'whether I might ask some of the old gang down for the weekend.'

Thomas's first reaction is one of dismay. He is by nature reclusive, a trait which has been encouraged by his upbringing, and the thought of the effort required to entertain people for a whole weekend is daunting. Being a reasonable man, however, he can understand that Clarissa will not wish to lose touch with her friends completely. He mumbles something into the shirt which he is pulling over his head whilst Clarissa, curled up in bed, sips at her coffee.

She senses that he is not absolutely overwhelmed with excitement at the prospect but she pushes on with her proposal. 'I thought you might like to see the Radcliffes again,' she suggests. 'They were so good to you in London, weren't they?'

She has touched a nerve. Charlie and Caroline *were* very good to him after Claerwen's death, inviting him to stay, listening to him, encouraging him.

'Sound man, Charlie,' he says, sitting down to lace up his shoes. 'We were at school together.'

'And we mustn't forget that it was Charlie and Caroline,' says Clarissa archly, 'who brought us together.'

Thomas smiles at her affectionately. 'How could I possibly forget?' he asks. 'Of course we must ask them down but perhaps,' he adds cunningly, 'we should mention it to the aunts first.'

He knows that the aunts are never keen to entertain – and why should they be? – and he hopes that there might be a few obstacles which are impossible to overcome. Clarissa bites back the comment that it is her house, too, remembering that she will not wish to be burdened with the catering and commissariat, and agrees to mention it to them.

'You haven't met any of my friends,' she muses, with just a touch of wistfulness.

Thomas, who can see no good reason for meeting his wife's friends, mumbles regretfully. Clarissa watches him, thoughtfully. She guesses that he would be more than content to go on exactly as they are, without ever leaving his estates or meeting any people beyond his own small circle. She remembers how she longed to show him off to her friends and begins to wonder whether it is a good plan after all. Will she be able to keep him awake after dinner? Will he understand their jokes? Will they find it odd that the entire household is in bed by eleven o'clock? Clarissa sighs. Thomas isn't *quite* the companion she'd hoped he'd be. Of course, there's always the house. They'll be green with envy when they see the house . . .

'Did the Radcliffes come when Claerwen was alive?' she asks casually.

'Charlie was my best man,' he says, 'and they stayed once or twice in the early days but not for years now. Claerwen couldn't cope with it, you see.'

Clarissa finishes her coffee and lifts her cheek for his kiss.

'Is the house haunted, Thomas?' she asks with pretended indifference.

He looks down at her, puzzled. 'Haunted?'

Irritation rises again. 'Yes. You know? Haunted? Ghosts and things? Spooks? Spirits? Shades? Things that go bump in the night?'

He always finds her funny when she's in this mood. 'Honestly, darling. Of course it isn't. Don't be silly.'

She is comforted by his amusement but presses him. 'No dear old ancestors hanging about?'

'Oh I see what you mean. You've been talking to Megan

and the aunts. They claim to see and hear all sorts of things but I think some of it is imagination. Of course, it's a very old house. Hundreds of people have lived and died here. It's bound to leave an atmosphere, I suppose. Certainly nothing to worry about, I promise you.'

His matter-of-factness has a very positive effect on her. Her spirits rise, her fear recedes and she smiles with relief. 'I think I love you,' she says, regretting her earlier irritation.

He beams down at her. 'So I should think. See you later.'

Feeling relaxed, Clarissa stretches and laughs a little at her fears. She realises that she has over-reacted, has allowed herself to be affected by Megan's fancifulness. Of course the house has atmosphere – but it is hardly the Hammer House of Horrors. She yawns and glances at her watch; plenty of time for a snooze. She snuggles down, pulls the blankets round her ears and wonders which of her friends she will honour with an invitation.

As Thomas has foreseen, the aunts are not enthusiastic at Clarissa's proposals. They are too clever to let her see their reluctance. On the contrary, they greet the plan with a show of delight but, when Clarissa retires to the book-room to write letters, they withdraw to the kitchen to discuss it privately. It is rather like judging when to allow a boy home from prep school in his first term. If it is too early it can do a great deal of harm; the family bonds reassert themselves before the new ties have been allowed to form securely. Will the old friends make Clarissa discontented with her new quiet, uneventful life? Will she be drawn back to her familiar ways?

'If she were pregnant,' says Aunt Gwyneth impatiently, 'I would feel more confident.'

'If she were pregnant,' says Aunt Olwen grimly, 'she probably wouldn't be bothering about old friends.'

'The Radcliffes are not a problem,' says Aunt Gwyneth confidently. 'They see and feel nothing. They are no threat either, being an older married couple, but as to these girlfriends . . .'

'They will explore,' says Aunt Olwen warningly. 'They will poke their noses into things that don't concern them . . .'

There is a small silence.

'It is too soon,' says Aunt Gwyneth firmly. 'She has not settled yet.'

'These friends,' says Aunt Olwen slowly. 'I wonder how close they really are. Apart from one or two telephone calls there seems to be very little contact.'

'They probably will not wish to come all this way simply to be made envious,' says Aunt Gwyneth shrewdly.

'On the other hand,' says Aunt Olwen thoughtfully, 'we don't want her becoming bored and restless.'

They stare at each other.

'This is very tiresome,' says Aunt Gwyneth crossly.

'I think we must allow it,' says Aunt Olwen reluctantly. 'They must come and they must enjoy themselves . . .'

'But not too much,' interrupts Aunt Gwyneth. 'The last thing we want is a stream of visitors. This is not an hotel . . . Hush!'

'Haven't seen the cat for ages,' says Nan Ellis coming in through the garden door. 'What's happened to it?'

The aunts' eyes meet and slide away.

'It has completely disappeared,' says Aunt Olwen. 'It was a feral cat, you know. They do as they please.'

'Funny, isn't it?' says Nan, approaching the sink and rolling up her sleeves. 'Can't keep a pet for two minutes in this house. Get a cat round the place and a few weeks later it's gone.'

'We're not pet people,' says Aunt Gwyneth. 'And the woods come close to the house. There are predators in the woods.'

'Predators?' Nan looks at her, head cocked, hands stilled, her native superstition well in evidence. 'What, foxes and things?'

'Of course,' nods Aunt Olwen. 'Foxes. Boar. Savage wild dogs. Huge cats. The woods are ancient. Who knows what they shelter?'

Nan shivers. 'Wouldn't catch me going in those old woods,' she says. 'My *nain* used to tell me all sorts of stories when I was small. Always told me to keep clear of the woods at night.'

'Ah,' says Aunt Gwyneth smiling. 'A wise woman, your *nain*. I remember her. She used to work for our mother.'

Nan sighs. ''Til she had that funny stroke. Couldn't speak afterwards. My da said she'd been struck dumb by the fairies for talking too much.'

She laughs at the recollection and the aunts laugh with her, heartily.

'Midsummer, it was,' remembers Nan. 'there was a bit of a to-do because little Owen went missing. Queer in his head he was and some said he'd fallen in the river. All sorts of talk there was and that very day a message comes down from your Ma saying that my *nain* had been struck down. Funny, it was. My da said that Owen had been taken by the gypsies. No-one ever saw him again.'

'Your da was a clever man,' says Aunt Olwen, after a moment. 'He looked after you so well. Your mother dead and your *nain* speechless and paralysed. He was a brave man. He brought you up to us as soon as you were old enough to work and said he knew we'd look after you.'

'Lucky to have the work in those days,' says Nan. 'Stuck out here, miles from anywhere.'

The aunts leave her to her washing-up and go into the hall. There are several letters lying on the hall table ready for the postman to collect. Three of the envelopes are addressed in Clarissa's hand and the aunts study the addresses carefully. An idea drifts into their heads and, after a moment, their eyes meet questioningly. The postman's van can be heard approaching and the aunts glance towards the door. He is here, getting out, whistling between his teeth as he comes up the steps . . .

Clarissa comes running down the stairs. 'Did I hear the postman?' she demands. 'Has he taken my letters?'

'Safely gone,' beams Aunt Olwen. 'What luck he has some post for us today. Here's one for you, look. All the way from America. What a pretty stamp.'

'Oh, goodie,' says Clarissa, 'it's from Georgy. My really, *really* best friend.'

The aunts nod and smile tolerantly; really, *really* best friends a long way off in America are the best sort to have.

'You go and sit by the fire in the small saloon and read it quietly,' says Aunt Gwyneth, 'and we'll bring you coffee with some of Aunt Olwen's shortbread. You'd like that? You would? Good girl.'

They vanish away kitchenwards and Clarissa smiles after them. What darling old things they are! Sighing with satisfaction and expectation she goes into the small saloon – no ghosts here today – and sits down by the fire. When the aunts appear with the tray of goodies, she is staring into the flames. The aunts exchange a glance.

'Not bad news, I hope?' asks Aunt Olwen, absentmindedly brushing the Little One away. This room has always been a favourite with him. 'You look so solemn.'

Clarissa looks round at them. She shakes her head and indicates the letter. 'I can't believe this. I simply can't believe it. Georgy's gone and got married. *Married*. To an American.'

The aunts are silent for a moment.

'Perhaps we shouldn't believe everything we hear about colonials,' says Aunt Olwen at last. 'We have several distant cousins who have done very well in Canada.'

'But she'll be so far away,' cries Clarissa. 'I'll never see her. Anyway . . .'

The 'anyway' hangs discontentedly on the air. The aunts know very well that Clarissa is slightly cross that her really, *really* best friend is married. *She* wanted to be the one to be envied and made much of and now this Georgy has gone and done it too. She has stolen some of Clarissa's thunder.

'Anyway,' goes on Clarissa sulkily, 'she might at least have told me. It's just come out of the blue. She could have written.'

'Perhaps it was very sudden,' guesses Aunt Gwyneth. 'Swept off her feet. Oh, dear.' She shakes her head. 'I hope she hasn't been rash.'

Clarissa brightens a little.

'Or,' offers Aunt Olwen, 'could it be that she is . . . obliged to marry. Not,' she hastens to add, 'that I am suggesting that your friend isn't . . .' She hesitates and sighs. 'It can happen to the nicest girls.'

Clarissa stares at the aunts. She realises that she doesn't want Georgy to be the first of their little group to become a mother. *She* has been the first to marry; she should be the first to produce the next generation. She has longed to do the motherhood bit – and now it seems that Georgy, who has always been so despising of Clarissa's maternal yearnings, might get there first.

The aunts exchange another glance and Aunt Olwen pours some coffee and carries it to Clarissa. 'Friends can be so thoughtless,' she murmurs. 'Insensitive and selfish. It's too bad.'

Clarissa sniffs a little. Georgy *has* been thoughtless and selfish; no warnings, no photographs, no invitation to the wedding. She remembers how she kept her really, *really* best friend in touch with every little detail from the first moment she met Thomas. She takes the coffee wondering how quickly she might become pregnant and how quickly she can dispatch the news to America. There is a strange silence in the room, a drifting current of cold air, and for some reason she thinks of Megan and her story of the Little One. She glances round quickly, nervously. The aunts are watching her, their strange grey eyes bright and keen.

'Drink up,' says Aunt Olwen gently. 'Have some shortbread. Don't worry about anything.'

'All will be well,' agrees Aunt Gwyneth. 'You'll see.'

6

Clarissa feels very hurt when her girlfriends don't reply to her invitations. Caroline Radcliffe telephones to say that they are rather tied up at the moment, maybe later in the year and so on, but from her other two friends there is nothing. She stomps about feeling rejected and cross and snaps at Thomas when he suggests that she should telephone them to sort it out. 'Why should I go crawling to them?' she cries.

Realising that this is a rhetorical question Thomas wisely makes no attempt to answer it.

'If,' she says loftily, 'they are so rude that they can't even be bothered to answer my letter then I have no desire to see them.'

Thomas remains silent. Clarissa is doing very nicely without his input and he can see that it is unlikely that the peaceful tenor of his life will be disturbed by chattering women. Events continue to favour his reclusiveness. When these very friends telephone to ask how Clarissa is and why they haven't heard from her for so long, it happens that she is out walking or in the bath and the aunts are able to explain that she has rather lost contact with her old life, implying that her new life is much more exciting. The chums are hurt when they discover that the Radcliffes have been invited but they haven't and there is a certain lessening of affection. Clarissa's popularity suffers a severe decline. Those few who are more persistent write to Clarissa but somehow these letters get as far as the hall and no farther. The aunts are watchful, encouraging Clarissa in her feeling that her life is now here with Thomas and that she needs no outside distractions. The idea of being a mother becomes more and more attractive.

Getting pregnant, however, isn't nearly so easy as Clarissa imagines. After nearly fifteen years of the Pill her body has some adjusting to do and she becomes more and more anxious, leaping on Thomas at every possible opportunity and becoming utterly obsessed with the idea of mother-hood. The more it eludes her the more she wants it. When Christmas comes and there is still no sign of life growing within her, she becomes quite desperate. She makes charts, takes her temperature and sticks her legs up the wall after intercourse; it has long ceased to be true love-making or even simple lust. Thomas feels used and is extremely tired. He thinks that he is looked upon solely as a baby-maker and he becomes resentful. To begin with it was rather fun. Claerwen had never suggested that they should make love in the airing cupboard or on the bathroom floor and especially not – a breathlessly athletic moment, this one – on the revolving chair in his business-room one afternoon just before tea. Now, however, he sees her so-called passion for what it is and he is faintly repelled by such a business-like approach.

Sensing discord the aunts attempt to distract Clarissa a little. They take her shopping to the nearest big town nearly forty miles away and she sits in the back of the car, like a child being taken for a treat. The countryside is wild and inhospitable but beautiful. Tiny fields cling to the steep sides of the mountains whose crags are white with snow. It seems that the cattle and the sheep must tumble off the sheer slopes into the rocky river-bed far below. As she sits watching the countryside unreel itself she wonders why she has allowed these two old dears to take control of her life. Surely *she* should be driving *them*? *She* should be the one in charge, organising and planning and allowing them to sink back into old age. Clarissa yawns and settles more comfortably, quite content for them to have the ordering of the day. She is too idle to make decisions or to take over the running of the house. Life is very comfortable – if dull – the way it is and she likes being pampered. Thomas has been a little less tolerant of late and the aunts' sympathy is very comforting . . .

She sits up a little as the car swerves and she hears a cry and a grinding of metal. Peering out of the window she sees a cyclist scrabbling about on the grass verge.

'Oh dear,' Aunt Olwen is saying. 'We've knocked him off his bicycle. Should we stop? He might be hurt.'

'Silly man wobbled right in front of me,' says Aunt Gwyneth, grinding gears. 'He's perfectly all right. I barely touched him.' She peers in the rear-view mirror. 'Nothing to worry about. He's getting up, not hurt at all. Look. He's waving at us.'

Glancing out of the back window Clarissa sees that this is perfectly true. He is waving both his fists as he dances up and down in the road. She slides down in her seat feeling a little embarrassed and hoping that he has not made a mental note of the number plate. She watches more anxiously as they approach the outskirts of the town but Aunt Gwyneth brings them safely to the car park and the aunts guide her into their favourite café so as to restore themselves with coffee. It is a charming place with its oak beams, panelled walls, and delicious home-made cakes set out on pretty flowered plates. Clarissa chooses a slice of lemon sponge and looks about her appreciatively.

The aunts watch her, glad to see that she is more calm of late, less agitated about her inability to conceive. They have decided that she has been getting too worked up about the whole thing and that she needs to relax a little. After all, it is still early days yet. The new tisane, which they have persuaded her to take at bedtime, is working wonders. In common with many other people, Clarissa believes that anything made from herbs and flowers must be quite harmless. The aunts find this a novel viewpoint, so many of nature's products are perfectly lethal, but this touching faith makes life much easier for them. They beam at her as she sips at her coffee whilst they consult their shopping list, murmuring together.

A man sitting at a table in the corner with an attractive woman is also watching them. Presently he stands up and comes over to their table. He is a handsome, casual-looking fellow in his forties, with blue eyes and fair hair, and Clarissa sits up a little straighter as he greets the aunts. They look delighted to see him and introduce him. Evan Lewis, a kinsman of some kind. They are somewhat vague about the actual relationship and his smile widens as he shakes Clarissa's hand. There is another of those odd little silences that Clarissa is beginning to get used to and, when Evan returns to his companion, Clarissa's eyes follow him appreciatively. He is tall – much taller than Thomas – and he has long straight legs and a really great bum . . .

Clarissa pulls herself together and looks at the aunts with a quick defensive smile. They are smiling too, as if they are filing away some useful fact for future use, and she takes a quick gulp at her coffee, glad that they aren't looking shocked. In fact they look quite naughty, as if they guess her thoughts and are encouraging her. Their eyes are bright, their cheeks rosy and she can't help grinning at them. Just for a moment it is like being out with the old chums and giggling over some sexy chap. When Evan leaves he raises a hand to them and there is a smile about his eyes which Clarissa finds faintly disturbing. She finds herself thinking about him whilst she shops and during the journey home, and she is a little more lively than she has been of late. Thomas might have become somewhat immune to her charms but it is clear that she is still an attractive woman; Evan's expression has made that very clear.

As the car turns in at the gate, Clarissa is struck anew by the beauty of the house and its setting. She remembers how she longed to show it off to her friends but now, somehow, it doesn't seem to matter any more. It is hers, that is what is important; hers and her children's . . . A twinge of dissatisfaction twists inside her. Supposing she can't have children? It never occurred to her that she wouldn't become pregnant the moment she decided to; that it wouldn't happen quite naturally and at once. The aunts assure her that she must give it time and that being anxious will only make it more difficult. She sighs, discontent making a brief come-back. Georgy didn't need time; poor old Georgy got caught out. She has heard more fully now from her really, *really* best friend. Things aren't going too well for poor old Georgy and Clarissa has forgiven her for that earlier imagined thoughtlessness. Poor old Georgy has got nearly everything wrong and Clarissa feels just the tiniest bit smug as the car chugs up the drive with the two darling old aunts together in the front. She feels another surge of confidence; soon she will be pregnant and then she will have everything her heart could desire.

When Megan arrives home for the Easter holidays Thomas greets her with something like relief; relief and a deeper appreciation of her spiritual qualities. He remembers how gentle and undemanding her mother was and experiences a genuine twinge of remorse. Beside her pale, delicate memory, Clarissa is somewhat larger than life and perhaps rather . . . vulgar? He remembers with shame how quickly after Claerwen's death he was seduced by Clarissa's charms.

There is something humiliating about being so susceptible to the temptations of the flesh and, looking back, he cannot quite recall why he found Clarissa so bewitching. At present she is behaving rather like a tart . . . Thomas pulls himself together, shocked at his thoughts and reminding himself that she is merely frustrated and unhappy because she cannot conceive. He is safe in the knowledge that it is not *his* fault – there is Megan to prove his manliness and the memories of the three miscarriages that poor Claerwen suffered during the years after Megan's birth. He smiles fondly upon his daughter, seeing how like her dear mother she is, approving the qualities which turn her thoughts into spiritual channels.

Clarissa is pleased to see Megan, too. She is such a sweet, unworldly child and she is so easy and natural. She can be a little unnerving at times but Clarissa is gradually becoming used to the strange atmosphere of the old house. Even the idea of the ghosts is slowly ceasing to alarm her. She feels too lethargic to worry about anything much. One afternoon, feeling in need of fresh air, she wanders outside in the warm spring sunshine. She strolls towards the back of the house and into the wood. Until now, she has found the place oppressive. In the summer, the dense foliage made it dark and airless and in the early winter it was muddy and wet underfoot. She prefers to walk beneath the trees that border the drive and stretch away to the fields. Now, on this bright spring day, however, the wood looks more welcoming. The leaves are only just beginning to uncurl, the sun pours in between the branches and the earth is dry and hard beneath her feet. She wanders deeper in, where the trees crowd close and presently the path disappears. She feels that she is being drawn along, following some unseen, ancient way, until now, deep in the woods, she sees the standing stones.

There is a strange silence here. No birds sing and no breeze stirs in the tree-tops. Slowly she moves into the circle where the grass is bright and thick and she stands for a moment, her head bent, the sun hot on her shoulders. As she stands, it seems to her that the space is slowly filling up around her, unseen presences press on every side. Her heart begins to pound with slow heavy strokes and she longs to kneel, to abase herself to something or someone powerful and terrible. Cries and whispers fill her ears. She groans aloud, resisting these strange forces, struggling helplessly against the weight which forces her to her knees but, as she falls, Megan bursts out of the trees behind her, seizing her arm and pulling her up and away from the stone circle.

Dazed, she stumbles with Megan out of the woods, gasping for air, her head pounding. Not until they are in the cool spacious gravelled court beside the house do they stop to pause for breath. Clarissa shakes her head to clear away the noises and clutches at Megan who still holds her arm.

'What was it?' she asks breathlessly. 'I came over all peculiar. It was . . . weird.'

'You were in the ancient grove where the Druids worshipped,' says Megan quite prosaically. 'It's full of powerful magic. You need to be . . .' she hesitates; 'armed,' she says at last.

Clarissa stares at her. 'Armed?' She has a vision of guns and knives.

'Strange things have happened there.' Megan fears that they still do but does not wish to frighten Clarissa too much. 'It's best to stay away from it. I never go there.'

'Then how did you know I was there?' asks Clarissa, puzzled and still very shaken. 'If you don't go there?'

'I saw you,' says Megan simply.

'Saw . . . ?' Clarissa rubs her head. She cannot cope with all this talk of magic and Druids, let alone Megan's own particular form of witchcraft. For one mad moment she longs to be back in the cramped flat in Fulham with busy, noisy London roaring in a normal, sane way outside the door.

'Come,' says Megan gently. 'I shall make you some tea. You are safe now. Come inside and sit down quietly.'

Sitting in the small saloon, Clarissa feels the urge to laugh hysterically. Only Megan would consider it safe and relaxing to sit in a room seething with spirits. She looks about, wondering how many of them are sharing the sofa with her. Her experience in the stone circle has left her feeling weak and light-headed and a sense of detachment sweeps over her, a kind of 'if you can't beat them, join them' sensation. She has married into a family of mad people whose ancestors have worshipped in their own personal Druids' grove and who still hang about the house three hundred years later – but what the hell?

'Hi,' she says languidly to the other occupants of the room. 'How are things?'

She wonders now if she imagined the whole thing; simply had a dizzy turn with the sun beating so hotly on her head. Perhaps she's pregnant, after all . . . Even this thought cannot rouse her from this strange, exhausted lethargy and, when Megan appears with the tea, Clarissa is fast asleep against the cushions.

As their first anniversary draws nearer, Clarissa is still not pregnant and Thomas has begun to decline into the quiet reclusive ways of his life before Clarissa. His brief flash of passion has burnt itself out and he is content to settle back into the daily round. Thomas works hard on his land and the spring and summer make demands on his time and energy. Discontent nibbles once more at the edge of Clarissa's herbally-induced languor. Even the aunts are beginning to feel anxious. If no child has been conceived whilst Clarissa is calm and Thomas has still been relatively energetic, what chance will there be now? Thomas snores away what remains of his evenings in front of the television and then retires sleepily to his dressing-room. He will be rising in the early dawn and does not wish to disturb Clarissa.

As May-day approaches the aunts are determined to make a very special occasion of the most important of the druidical festivals: Beltane. Down the centuries the old heathen ways have become distorted and confused but the aunts know that the fire festivals were important for all sorts of reasons and sacrifice was a major part of them. They sigh with frustration when they think how easy it was for their ancestors. Even quite recently, in the time of dear Mama, there wasn't all this fuss if unwanted people

– half-witted children, passing tramps and so on – not to mention various forms of livestock, simply disappeared. The locals put it down to the gypsies or the fairies and that was that. Nowadays – the aunts shake their heads and click their tongues impatiently – everyone's a member of Neighbourhood Watch or they're glued to that terrible programme – what's it called? Crimewatch? – so that there isn't a moment's peace. They remind each other of a very nasty moment – what thirty, forty years ago? – when a lost and luckless hitch-hiker dropped in for a glass of water on Midsummer's Eve and then disappeared. They still wonder whether dear Mama saw him as being sent direct from the Goddess and acted accordingly. Unfortunately some nosey person had seen him in the lane near the house and it had required some very clever footwork to deflect the local policeman elsewhere. The aunts chuckle a little together as they remember; you had to be up early to get the better of dear Mama. How ruthless she'd been, how dedicated. They wonder if their failure to find an heiress to the house and the grove is because they have not the courage and fierceness of dear Mama and her ancestors.

They begin their preparations for May-day's Eve which they still think of as Walpurgis Night. Gradually they collect together enough dry wood to build a respectable bonfire on the open slopes behind the grove and brood upon a sacrifice. It is a pity that Thomas has given up on having dogs about the place but the aunts shrug philosophically. Well, they were nasty little brutes, always covered in fleas or trying to mount one's leg, and dispatching them had caused the aunts no twinge of regret. Thomas, always so naive and gullible, has been easy to convince and he believes that the dogs were stolen or got lost whilst out hunting on the mountains. It is odd, think the aunts, that the legitimate sons of the family are so unimaginative and slow whilst those born on the wrong side of the blanket . . .

As the memory of Evan Lewis smiling at Clarissa comes into their minds the aunts exchange a thoughtful glance. He is, after all, a Mortimer; perhaps the time has come to make a small diversion. It seems unlikely that Clarissa, personally, is going to enter into the true life of the house and the grove – she is disappointingly squeamish – but she is their only hope at present of providing the future custodian. If Thomas won't oblige then someone else must do his work for him and Evan is a near – a very near – relation, descended from powerful women. The thought spurs them on and they make a very great effort for the Goddess on this special occasion. So it is that several small wild animals, as well as a villager's promiscuous and tiresome tom cat, find themselves on an unexpected outing on the eve of May-day and the aunts return to the house alone in the early hours, weary but content. The Goddess is appeased and will continue to protect them.

It seems, therefore, to be a puzzling part of some yet-to-be revealed plan when, a few days later, Thomas overturns a tractor in the plantation on the steep hillside. He is trapped for hours before help arrives and his legs are badly crushed. He is to remain in hospital for several months and it seems that he will be confined to a wheelchair for some time, if not forever. Clarissa, jolted out of her somnolence by this tragedy, spends most days travelling between the house and the hospital which is on the outskirts of the town forty miles away. She is shocked to find that she is almost enjoying the drama and realises that in Thomas's absence the house seems more completely hers. She feels full of energy, suddenly; useful and necessary. The hospital staff are full of admiration at her cheerful bravery in such tragic circumstances and she is able to be tender and loving and encouraging to poor Thomas, whilst enjoying their approbation.

It's such a happy coincidence that Evan Lewis happens to be in the building trade. It is the aunts who think of him when it becomes clear that alterations will have to be made before Thomas comes home again. He will need the use of several rooms on the ground floor and ramps must be built to accommodate the wheelchair.

'It must be done carefully,' says Clarissa anxiously. 'We mustn't spoil the house . . .'

She stops, feeling ashamed. What is a house compared to poor Thomas's comfort? The aunts are nodding approvingly, however. They quite agree with her. Moreover, the house is listed so caution must be exercised.

'In that case we need someone who knows all the rules and regulations,' says Clarissa. 'It will probably be very expensive. Do you know a local builder?'

The aunts look a little vague; each seems unwilling to meet the other's eye as they feel the hand of the Goddess upon them. They purse their lips and frown a little and it is Aunt Olwen who suddenly exclaims, 'Of course, there's Evan Lewis. I think he's rather good.'

'Oh yes,' says Aunt Gwyneth. 'Evan. Now there's a thought.'

'Evan?' Clarissa is racking her memory. 'Didn't I meet him?'

'So you did!' cries Aunt Olwen, pleased. 'Now that's splendid. He's such a nice man. Didn't you think so? I don't think you'd mind having him about the place, would you?'

Clarissa is remembering his smile and his long legs – and her cheeks feel a little hot.

'It's so important,' Aunt Gwyneth is murmuring, 'that one likes the people about one. Workmen can be *rather* tiresome.'

'I'm sure we could trust Evan to be sensitive and accommodating,' says Aunt Olwen. 'He is, after all, one of the family so to speak.'

Clarissa looks at her curiously. 'I remember you said something about that once before,' she said. 'How . . . ? What . . . ? I mean . . .' She is too embarrassed to go on but the aunts are prepared to be quite open with her now.

'I'm afraid that the Mortimers have always been rather, shall we say *generous* with their favours,' says Aunt Gwyneth, beaming at her. 'The old *droit de seigneur*, as it were. A tiny bit naughty, I'm afraid, but you know how it is? We're only human, after all.'

Clarissa is enchanted by such an open-minded approach to life. Really, these old dears are just too terrific for words. All the same . . .

'Doesn't sound like Thomas,' she murmurs with a complicit little smile.

They laugh delightedly. Dear old Thomas, they agree, is the *least* bit strait-laced but then each family has its strange genetic brew and one never quite knows what each generation might produce . . . An odd silence falls.

Clarissa fiddles with her coffee cup. 'It seems that Thomas might not be able to . . . you know?' she says slowly. 'Perhaps I shall never have a child.'

The aunts hasten to comfort her.

'Don't count your chickens before they're hatched,' advises Aunt Gwyneth, filling Clarissa's cup with hot coffee.

'More than one way of killing a cat than drowning it in cream,' says Aunt Olwen, passing the shortbread. 'You just wait and see.'

Clarissa has the oddest feeling that something momentous is being suggested. She looks up to see the aunts watching her, the curiously light grey eyes bright and intelligent. She smiles at them and they sigh with relief. The Goddess works in strange and complex ways and who are they to question them? They feel magic moving in the air and beam confidently upon Clarissa. Everything is going simply splendidly.

*   *   *

This is not a sentiment which is shared by Thomas. He is no longer in pain, in fact he can feel nothing at all in the lower half of his body, but he feels that his life is as good as over. He is morose and unco-operative and the hospital staff become even more impressed by Clarissa's patient, loving care. She sits with him for hours, talking encouragingly about the work to be done at the house and telling him how much they are all looking forward to having him home. She holds his hand and brings him little gifts but he remains withdrawn. Even the aunts cannot help him out of his misery. Clarissa smiles bravely when the matron sympathises with her privately; she dabs at the corner of her eyes and her lips tremble a little when she says that she is determined to get Thomas walking again one day. The matron is rather sharp with Thomas when she returns to his room. She tells him that he mustn't wallow in self-pity and congratulates him on having two lovely aunts and a wonderful wife.

The aunts have gone on ahead to meet Evan for lunch. He is shocked at poor Thomas's plight and very ready to do what he can to make the house ready for his return home. It will, he warns, take rather a long time. He will have to speak to the planning department, obtain permission and so on, but first he will need to come out to the house and see exactly what is to be done. They assure him that there is no hurry to complete the work. It will be some time before Thomas can be allowed out of hospital.

If Evan is surprised that there is a distinct lack of depression at this thought on the part of Thomas's aunts he does not show it and when Clarissa arrives they all make a concerted effort to cheer her up. The lunch becomes an almost festive affair and when he says goodbye there is a definite atmosphere of friendliness between them all. The three of them drive home together, Aunt Olwen nearly knocking down a shopper who is foolhardy enough to cross the road on the zebra crossing. Clarissa wishes that she had insisted on driving but, after all, it *is* the aunts' car. As she stares back at the enraged shopper who has managed to leap to safety she is reminded of a joke. *There are only two types of pedestrian about when I'm driving; the quick and the dead.* She laughs silently and wishes she had someone with whom to share it. Perhaps Evan . . .

She allows herself to think about him. Apart from being drop-dead gorgeous he is such fun; just like the aunts, in fact, but not terribly like Thomas. That naughty sense of humour is quite missing from Thomas's character and comes as a welcome change after his morose coldness. She feels a little shiver of excitement at the thought of seeing him again – Evan, not Thomas – and is once more aware of the feeling that the aunts are conniving at the friendship.

When Evan turns up at the house, to take measurements and discuss what might be needed for Thomas, this feeling is strengthened. This is not the first time that he has been to the house, although it is a long while since he has been here, and it is clear that he is responding to the atmosphere. He walks from room to room, his face thoughtful and brooding. Clarissa watches him curiously, wondering if he is aware of the presence of the spirits. The aunts have hurried away to prepare tea and Clarissa does not have the courage to ask him what he can sense in this house of his ancestors. He looks almost forbidding, quite unapproachable, as he stands silently in the small saloon and Clarissa finds it impossible to utter the light-hearted remark which springs to mind. She is relieved when the aunts return, bringing with them an ease of manner along with the tea-tray.

It is Aunt Olwen who suggests that after Clarissa next visits Thomas she should meet up with Evan to see what progress is being made on the planning front. She says it so innocently, head on one side, eyes on Evan, and he agrees with a much less innocent glance at Clarissa. By then, he says, he might have some news regarding the permissions needed and he will have done some costing out. The aunts nod approvingly and Clarissa, with just the right amount of nonchalance, says that she will be quite happy to meet him. She waits for someone to think of the telephone as an excellent means of communication and is surprised at how relieved she is when it is not mentioned. They are all content, it seems, to wait until her next trip to town which, since she visits Thomas so regularly, will be very soon.

So it begins.

8

Even Megan cannot raise Thomas's spirits. Home for half-term, she spends nearly every possible moment at his bedside. Clarissa is very ready to drive her to the town. It is quite right and proper that the child should want to be with her father.

'It is important for Megan to be alone with him,' murmurs Clarissa to the matron. 'I don't want to interfere. I have so much opportunity to be with him and, after all,' she adds wistfully, 'I am only her *step*-mother.'

She desperately wishes that Thomas would respond, would re-assert himself as a strength in her life. She is being swept away on the current of her growing attachment to Evan and fears that she might have mistaken her feelings for Thomas. They are gentle pale emotions beside this new passion. What is more, the aunts seem to be encouraging her. Evan is amusing and kind, although she has seen that odd, dark side which appears in Thomas's character. There is one very important difference between the two men. Evan genuinely likes women. He is not, like Thomas, simply polite and gentle to them; he really likes and understands them – perhaps rather too much for his own good. He is naughty and flirtatious and fun and Clarissa finds him very difficult to resist. He is also sympathetic and kind; all-in-all a lethal combination. Clarissa is aware of the danger and hopes that

Megan may succeed with Thomas where she has failed. She is surprised at how pleased she is to see Megan, how fond of her she is. She wishes that Megan was truly her own child: there is a strength and constancy about her and she makes no attempt to monopolise Thomas or exclude Clarissa.

'She's such an unselfish child,' she whispers to Matron, 'but I am determined that she shall have quality time with her father. Perhaps *she* can help him,' she adds pathetically.

'Now none of that,' mutters Matron fiercely. 'You have been a *brick*, an absolute *brick*.'

Clarissa smiles gratefully but she is beginning to panic. As usual, her own strength is being sapped by those who are stronger than she is. The aunts and Evan are determined that she shall be comforted and, once Megan returns to school and Thomas continues to refuse to be encouraged, Clarissa is overwhelmed by her own needs. She sees now that her love for Thomas was simply a dress-rehearsal for the real thing and she feels guilty and exalted by turn. Evan is charmed by her barely disguised feelings for him and has no qualms at all in encouraging them.

Unfortunately, their joint passion consumes them before Clarissa has got herself sorted out; nor is Evan prepared. It seems that he has the same casual attitude as his ancestors when it comes to distributing his seed and, once she comes to her senses, Clarissa is terrified. She prays that she will be as infertile with Evan as she has been with Thomas and does some quick calculations in her head. If she is unlucky, might it be possible to pass the child off as Thomas's, conceived just before his accident? She doesn't have to be Einstein to discover that the answer is 'No'. Clarissa tries to laugh lightly at her fears. Having been unable to conceive after nearly a year of lawful love-making with her husband is it likely that she should succumb now, after just one mad moment of fornication? The answer this time is 'Yes'. Soon after midsummer she knows that she is with child.

The aunts know, too. They watch with interest as she becomes thinner and more preoccupied; they note her regular visits to the bathroom – and her disappointed face when she emerges – and her sudden passion for energetic walks. When she subconsciously clenches her fists they know she is raging against the cruelty of life; the bitter twist of fate. When it seems that she might actually consider harming the unborn child – lots of gin, *very* hot baths, violent exercise – they decide to intervene.

They corner her one afternoon in the drawing-room – they pronounce it 'droin-room' – and ask her if anything is wrong. She sits well back in the corner of the sofa, clutching a cushion to her breast, staring at them with frightened eyes.

'I'm pregnant,' she blurts. 'Oh, God. Can you believe it? Pregnant,' and waits for the kind enquiry on their faces to turn to shock and disgust.

They beam at her as if she is a particularly clever child, exclaiming with delight, and she realises that they think it is Thomas's baby. She closes her eyes and prays for guidance. Can she attempt to deceive them? She knows that they will soon realise the terrible truth so she might as well come right out with it.

'It is not Thomas's child,' she says loudly and clearly – but hesitates over naming Evan. She cannot quite bring herself to do that, somehow.

The aunts nod understandingly. So what? their smiles seem to say. A mere technicality. Who cares? A baby is a baby.

Clarissa gazes at them uncomprehendingly. Have they not understood her? 'It's *not* . . .' she begins again – but they shake their heads dismissively.

'Of course not,' says Aunt Olwen. 'It doesn't matter. It is a very special baby.'

'So long awaited,' agrees Aunt Gwyneth fervently.

Clarissa stares at them fearfully. Are they losing their marbles at last? What can they mean by long awaited? Perhaps they think she has been chosen as an instrument for the Second Coming?

'How d'you mean?' she asks anxiously. 'Long awaited?'

They look at her with some surprise, realise the danger and pat her soothingly. They do not wish her to become suspicious.

'You've wanted a baby for nearly a year,' points out Aunt Olwen mendaciously. 'This is wonderful news.'

'I wanted *Thomas's* baby,' shouts Clarissa. 'This is . . . This is . . .'

'Evan's baby,' supplies Aunt Gwyneth comfortably. 'Never mind. She will be a Mortimer.'

'She?' questions Clarissa, thrown off her stride by the confidence of Aunt Gwyneth's prediction. 'Hang on. Aren't you even cross? About me and Evan?'

They laugh gently together. They never question the ways of the Goddess but it is clear that they need to calm Clarissa.

'You are young and pretty,' says Aunt Olwen, 'and you have no husband, so to speak. Evan is tall and handsome . . .'

'And has a wife,' says Clarissa drily. 'We mustn't forget his wife.'

The aunts are inclined to dismiss the subject of the wife as irrelevant, she doesn't enter into their calculations, but Clarissa is becoming rather hysterical.

'He's got a wife,' she cries, 'and two children of his own. He'll *never* leave her and marry me.'

The aunts are momentarily silenced by such a pedestrian and middle-class idea.

'*Marry* you?' repeats Aunt Olwen after a moment. 'Why should he do that? You are already married to Thomas.'

Clarissa begins to weep quietly into the cushion and the

aunts exchange an anxious look. Clearly, pregnancy is going to make her peevish and irrational. They shake their heads at the tiresome morality of the modern girl: really, it is surprising that the youth of today have any fun at all.

'Come now,' says Aunt Gwyneth, gently stroking her hair. 'You would hate to be married to Evan. He may be handsome but he is a naughty boy in many ways. Just think of your lovely little girl and be thankful.'

Clarissa raises a distraught face from the cushion, whose beautiful, delicate embroidery wrought by the hand of some dear old ancestor is now covered with snot and tears, and stares at them beseechingly. 'Look,' she says, '*please* try to understand. How am I going to explain this to Thomas? We didn't make love for several weeks before his accident. He was always too tired. I cannot pass it off as his child unless we convince him that it needed nearly *twelve months in the womb*!'

She begins to weep again and Aunt Gwyneth carefully removes the cushion so as to preserve it from further harm.

'Well if that's what's troubling you why on earth didn't you say so?' asks Aunt Olwen, laughing. 'Silly girl. Dear Mama had exactly the same problem.'

Clarissa forgets to weep. She stares open-mouthed at the darling old aunts who sit smiling back at her. 'Your *mother* . . . ? *Your* mother . . . ?' She shakes her head. 'I can't believe this.'

'Darling Mama,' begins Aunt Gwyneth, 'was very naughty with Evan's grandfather. *Just* like Evan he was, you know. *Such* a good-looking man. But unluckily the child was conceived at a time when our dear father was away from home. So you see how history repeats itself?'

Clarissa nods, mesmerised. 'So what . . . ?'

'Well, dear Mama,' says Aunt Olwen, taking up the tale, 'went off to stay with her sister – who was most fortuitously ill – before our father noticed anything odd and she returned when she was quite fit again. Evan's grandfather took the child into his own home. His own wife had just had a stillborn child so it all turned out splendidly.'

'Splendidly,' agrees Clarissa, watching the aunts with a fascinated eye. 'And Evan's grandfather's wife didn't object?'

'People were not so squeamish in those days,' says Aunt Gwyneth firmly. 'She was very glad to have the child.'

'So Evan,' says Clarissa slowly, 'is . . . Good grief! Evan is your nephew. Christ! He's Thomas's cousin or something.'

'So you see,' says Aunt Olwen happily, 'it's all in the family. Nothing to worry about.'

'Except,' says Clarissa firmly, 'except that *I* haven't got a sister and I don't want Evan's wife to bring up *my* child.'

'Naturally not,' agrees Aunt Gwyneth patiently. 'We were simply showing you how difficulties can be overcome if only you have faith.'

Clarissa lays back limply in the corner of the sofa and closes her eyes. She cannot see or feel the presence of yet another dear old ancestor who died in an agonising child-birth and who now sits beside her on the sofa, communicating sympathy. The aunts glare at this shade, disapproving of anything that might give off negative waves.

'All will be revealed to us,' they say comfortingly. 'Rest assured, we shall be given a Sign.'

At this moment, the telephone begins to ring. Clarissa, whose nerves are in shreds, gives a faint scream and the aunts exchange another speaking glance and go hurrying out. They rather wish that darling Clarissa had a little more backbone and realise that their problems are far from over. Aunt Olwen lifts the receiver and a clear decisive voice speaks in her ear.

'Hello? I'd like to speak to Clarissa, please. Tell her it's Georgy.'

* * *

It is clear that Georgy is exactly what everyone has been waiting for. Never has a Sign been given so promptly. Clarissa leaps from the sofa and races out to speak to her really, *really* best friend whilst the aunts look at each other, brows raised. They listen unashamedly to the conversation taking place in the hall. There are long gaps whilst Clarissa listens intently and her replies indicate that all is not well.

'Oh *no*. Oh my *God*, I don't believe it . . . Poor Georgy . . . You *haven't*! You poor, poor thing. Look come straight home. Of *course* you can. There's simply masses of room here . . . Oh well, never mind all that. No, he's no better. Still in hospital . . . As a matter of fact – but look, I can't talk now. Just come. Honestly. It'd be simply heaven to have you here . . . You will? Fantastic . . . OK, but stay in touch . . . Another week? OK, I'll wait to hear from you. Now no more worrying. We'll look after you . . . I know, love you lots too. 'Bye.'

When she comes back into the room the aunts are waiting for her, ready with sympathy should it be needed.

Clarissa has no intention of keeping anything from them. 'Can you believe it?' she demands. 'Poor Georgy. This wretched man gets her into trouble, OK so he *does* marry her and then she finds he's got a wife and three kids in Seattle. It's the most *ghastly* muddle and the wife and kids turn up and everything and it seems that the marriage wasn't legal and *now* poor Georgy's lost the baby.'

The aunts are somewhat confused by this breathless recital but they are prepared to be shocked by poor Georgy's story and can already see one or two useful possibilities arising from it.

'I hope you told her,' says Aunt Olwen – as if she doesn't know it perfectly well – 'that she has a home here.'

'Well, I did,' says Clarissa, horrified by Georgy's plight whilst enjoying it all enormously. 'She lost her job when they found she was pregnant and she can't face the thought of telling her parents. They were so thrilled when she got the job and everything. Georgy's always been mega brilliant. Top of everything at school. Pretty. Terrific fun. Practical. It's simply not *like* her to get into such a muddle.'

The aunts sigh sympathetically.

'It will be good for you to have a friend with you just now,' says Aunt Gwyneth gently. 'It will take your mind off things.'

'Yes,' says Clarissa thoughtfully, wondering how to present her own little drama to Georgy without losing face. The aunts watch her, sensing her dilemma.

'She'll be so envious,' murmurs Aunt Olwen, 'to see your lovely home and darling Thomas so devoted, even if he is incapacitated at present.'

'Not to mention,' twinkles Aunt Gwyneth naughtily, 'a *rather* gorgeous lover and a lovely baby on the way. *Won't* she be jealous?'

Immediately the sordid aspects of the affair vanish and the whole thing seems rather glamorous and fun. Instead of feeling faintly grubby and ashamed Clarissa feels that she is, after all, perhaps an exciting person who knows how to live life to the full. She takes a deep breath and glances up; the aunts are watching her, those strange eyes bright. Suddenly she feels confident and happy. Everything will sort itself out somehow as long as she just goes with the flow.

'Poor old Georgy,' she says. 'She's rather mucked it up. Never mind. We'll look after her.'

The aunts relax and begin to bustle about, excited at the thought of a visitor, planning which room she shall have, refusing to let Clarissa worry about any of the arrangements.

'You must take care of yourself,' they tell her. 'We can't take any risks. You shall supervise but nothing strenuous.

First a little drink, perhaps? To celebrate the darling baby? You'd like that? You would? *Good* girl.'

Clarissa settles back on the sofa and almost wishes that she could see all the dear old ghosts. If they are anything like the darling aunts they must be simply heaven. She is beginning to feel that there is something rather comforting about the idea of having so much family back-up. Not like poor old Georgy . . . Smiling happily, she swings her feet up onto the sofa, waiting for her drink.

9

Georgy, thin, intense, alert, wins everyone's hearts. From the first moment she hits exactly the right note. When Clarissa meets her at the station she is rather shocked at first to see her friend looking so much older – but she is the same old Georgy and they hug each other madly, laughing with delight that they are together again.

'Darling, don't say a word,' says Georgy firmly. 'Not 'til I've got my breath. I simply cannot believe I'm here. I know I look like a hag, don't tell me. You, on the other hand, look simply blooming. Being married obviously suits you.'

'Yes,' says Clarissa hurriedly – Georgy is right, the railway station is no place for confidences. 'Do I? Come on, let's get you home.'

Georgy sinks back in the passenger seat and 'Oh, the utter bliss of it. Not to have to worry for a while. I'm exhausted,' she says and leaves the chattering to Clarissa until the car pulls in at the gate.

'Stop!' instructs Georgy sitting upright. 'Wait! Oh, wow. Really, *really* wow!' She stares at the house with gratifying amazement and awe. 'It's just . . . perfect,' she says slowly. 'Oh, Clarissa. You lucky, lucky girl.'

'It's rather nice, isn't it?' agrees Clarissa, casually, but she flushes when Georgy turns to look at her in surprise.

'Rather nice?' she repeats, almost contemptuously.

'OK,' says Clarissa, swiftly shedding her air of sophistication under Georgy's keen stare. 'It's fantastic. It's wonderful. I simply adored it from the first moment I saw it. I felt I could *kill* for it.'

Georgy's eyebrows shoot up at this unguarded revelation. 'Is that why you married him?' she asks lightly.

'Of *course* it isn't why I married him,' says Clarissa indignantly. 'Thomas is an absolute sweetie. But you have to admit it's a hell of a bonus.'

Georgy, however, is not fooled by Clarissa's denial and she is silent for a moment as she stares at the house.

'The garden isn't too impressive,' Clarissa is saying as the car proceeds slowly up the drive. She is delighted that the day is sunny but sorry that the great banks of rhododendrons have finished flowering. There are no herbaceous borders or climbing roses, no attempt at charm, so that the whole effect is one of strong simplicity. 'We're so near the mountains that it's difficult to grow things. We're above the snow line here.'

'I think it's very impressive,' says Georgy softly. 'It's not pretty, it's beautiful. And it's clever not to have tarted it up. You can see its lovely bones.'

Clarissa is delighted by Georgy's reaction and she feels the thrill and pride of ownership. She is not surprised by Georgy's intensity; Georgy has always felt things keenly.

'Wait 'til you meet the aunts,' she warns with a laugh. 'They're part of the set-up, too, remember.'

As the car sweeps round in front of the door the aunts appear, coming out on to the steps, smiling welcomingly. Georgy cranes to peer at them, still in their tweeds and jerseys even on this warm August day, and chuckles with delight.

'But they're just perfect,' she exclaims. 'They match the house exactly.'

She steps out of the car and goes round to meet them.

Clarissa makes the introductions and Georgy shakes the outstretched hands, noticing the firm grip and the searching looks from their bright grey eyes.

'But what shall I call you?' she asks, laughing. 'You're not *my* aunts, unfortunately.'

'We look upon you quite as one of the family,' says Aunt Olwen firmly. 'We are Aunt Olwen and Aunt Gwyneth. Now that's settled. No fuss, please. You must come in and have some luncheon.'

'Clarissa will show you your room,' says Aunt Gwyneth. 'Come down when you're ready.'

The girls carry the luggage upstairs, chattering happily together, watched by the aunts from the hall below.

'She seems a very sensible girl,' says Aunt Olwen thoughtfully.

'Just what we need at the moment,' agrees Aunt Gwyneth.

Their eyes meet and slide away.

'Time will tell,' murmurs Aunt Olwen.

They cross the hall together and disappear towards the kitchen.

It is not too long before Clarissa feels that nothing has changed since she and Georgy were at school together. Georgy's energy, her strength of character, her quickness to assess and calculate situations, all combine to make Clarissa feel the least bit slow, flat-footed and lazy. It doesn't matter, not a bit, she tells herself, because Georgy has this knack of looking after her, teasing her a little, but generally taking control. Clarissa likes it. In a way, of course, the aunts have done just this but it's fun to have Georgy to gossip with and to share her worries. The aunts are terrific, absolutely fantastic, but it's not quite the same as having someone of your own age to whom you can pour out your heart and with whom you can exchange secrets.

In fact, now that Georgy is here she says very little about

her experience in America. Although Clarissa is ready to share every ghastly detail, Georgy tends to shrug it off and turn the conversation back to Clarissa. She remembers now that it has always been so. At school Georgy was always much more interested – perhaps concerned is a better word? wonders Clarissa affectionately – about others. When she thinks about it, she discovers that she actually knows very little about her really, *really* best friend. Now that they have plenty of time together Clarissa attempts to discover more but Georgy again changes the subject back to Clarissa and there is something so seductive about being encouraged to talk about herself that she doesn't get very far at all.

Before long, Georgy has wormed the whole truth out of Clarissa. She is faintly surprised that Clarissa has shown so much enterprise and tells her so, rather admiringly. Clarissa, who has feared that Georgy might find it all faintly sordid, is delighted and relieved by her reaction.

'You clever old thing,' says Georgy, strolling over to look out of the bedroom window – Clarissa is suffering terribly with morning sickness and rises late – 'acquiring houses, husbands, lovers, babies, even the aunts. I'm green with jealousy.'

Propped against the pillows, sipping iced orange juice, Clarissa feels a glow of achievement. She *has* been rather resourceful now she comes to think about it and she simpers deprecatingly. 'Oh well,' she says. 'You have to look out for yourself in this life.'

'Too true,' says Georgy, still at the window, observing Evan who has just arrived. 'So how are you going to get the baby past Thomas?'

Clarissa shifts uncomfortably and looks miserable. Her sense of achievement fades rapidly. 'Don't,' she says. 'Honestly, I feel ill with terror sometimes. Thank God he can't come home just yet. The aunts are so casual about it all but I simply don't know what to do.'

Georgy has already had a long and illuminating talk with the aunts but she is not quite ready yet to put forward her own ideas.

'I'm longing to meet Evan,' she says, coming back to sit on the end of the bed. 'He starts work here today, doesn't he?'

Although she misses his warmth and humour terribly, Clarissa feels too ill these days to be capable of sustaining any physical passion for Evan. Guilt and confusion have tainted her love and ruined her happiness. She looks hunted and slides down lower beneath the quilt. 'I simply can't face him,' she says. 'Of course he doesn't know about the baby. You won't say anything . . . ?' Her voice edges up towards panic. 'Oh, I don't know what to do. I feel so exhausted . . .'

'Don't get in a state,' advises Georgy, soothingly. 'I have a feeling that everything is going to be just fine.'

'Do you?' asks Clarissa, longing to be convinced. 'But how?'

'Trust me,' says Georgy. 'Try to sleep a little. I'll pop in later. I should stay put with Evan around. Better not see him while you're looking so awful.'

Clarissa feels a sense of frustration. She longs to feel free and lively, as she did whilst she was visiting Thomas in hospital and meeting Evan in his little flat, but she also wants to sink into some dark, warm sea of forgetfulness. She feels a tiny stab of jealousy that Georgy is swinging out of the door, tall, thin, vital, attractive, whilst she huddles lumpily and frowstily in bed. She wonders what Evan will think of Georgy and feels another twinge of jealousy. 'Stay,' she begs. 'Stay and talk to me.'

'Don't be silly, sweetie,' chides Georgy. 'You need rest. Plenty of time for chats. Back soon.'

The door closes behind her and Clarissa gives a sob of misery.

'I don't want a baby,' she mutters. 'I don't *want* it.' Immediately she is filled with a violent surge of bilious dizziness, rather as if the occupant of her womb is protesting. Clarissa is swamped with more guilt. 'Sorry,' she mutters feebly. 'Sorry.' Propping herself up a little she sips at the concoction the aunts have made for the relief of the nausea and then falls back against the pillows. As the sickness recedes and she slips into drowsiness she wonders how Georgy is getting on with Evan.

Georgy is getting on very well indeed. She has the opportunity to observe him for a moment whilst he is talking to the aunts but they quickly sense her presence and she is obliged to go forward to be introduced. The aunts watch them closely as they shake hands and are well aware of the undercurrent of quick attraction and recognition between two people who like to have their own way.

'Such a pity that dear Thomas will have to be confined,' sighs Aunt Olwen, once Evan and Georgy have murmured polite greetings. 'The trouble with such an old house is that there are so many different levels.'

'We're lucky to get permission to do anything at all,' Evan points out.

'At least the two rooms are fairly large,' says Aunt Gwyneth, 'and the morning-room has French windows to the garden.'

'Clarissa is determined to get him walking again,' says Georgy brightly. 'So it won't be for ever.'

A sliding glance passes between the other three and Evan whistles softly between his teeth.

'Perhaps,' says Aunt Olwen, 'perhaps for the time being it will be sensible if he is not too . . . adventurous.'

Evan smiles to himself and looks up to see Georgy watching him. He stares back at her.

'Will it take long?' she asks. 'Have you got minions or are

you going to do it all on your own? You don't look like a builder but I see you drive a Porsche. Perhaps you're what is called a Property Developer?'

He continues to stare at her, amused but refusing to be drawn.

'As a favour to us,' says Aunt Olwen, faintly reprovingly but enjoying the challenge of Georgy's question, 'Evan is going to do the work himself. He knows how we hate having strangers in this house.'

'Gosh!' says Georgy at once. 'I hope that's not a dig at me! Shall I go and pack?'

The aunts laugh at her naughtiness, she rather reminds them of dear Mama, and shake their heads at her.

'You're one of the family now,' they tell her. 'Just like Evan. And what would dear Clarissa do without you?'

'What indeed?' asks Georgy, her eyes on Evan's. 'Especially now.'

'How is Clarissa?' asks Evan smoothly. 'Still suffering with morning sickness?'

Georgy laughs. She might have guessed that the aunts would have told him everything.

'She is indeed,' she says cheerfully. 'Prostrated with it.'

The aunts cluck sympathetically but Evan continues to smile.

'Thomas must be so proud,' he murmurs. 'The luck of it and him helpless now. Confined to a wheelchair and two rooms. Surely the thought of the child will comfort him in his frustration.'

For once Georgy can think of no quick suitable answer and he laughs out loud as he goes down the passage to the side door. The aunts are smiling, too.

'Of course, he has Megan,' says Georgy gently. 'She must be a great comfort to him. But what does Megan think about . . . all this?'

There is a silence. Evan pauses, his hand on the door-handle, and the aunts frown.

'So quick to notice things, girls of that age,' muses Georgy. 'They ask such direct questions. She'll want to talk it over with her father, I expect. A new baby is always so exciting. Megan must be looking forward to having a step-brother or sister. I'm really longing to meet her,' and she beams at them as she turns away to go back upstairs to Clarissa.

Megan is in retreat at the convent. Thomas has given his permission for her to enter the convent as a postulant as soon as she is old enough to leave school. No-one has argued with him and Megan is quietly radiant. The aunts are actually relieved and Clarissa no longer has the energy, or the certainty, to fight it out with him.

'The nuns believe that she might have a vocation,' he says firmly. 'Her mother would have wished it for her. There will be time enough to see if they are right. It is not easy to become a nun, you know. Megan has a long hard road ahead.'

As she climbs the stairs, Georgy ponders on Megan and wonders whether she will notice anything at all. Clarissa has told her how dreamy and other-worldly she is, although she has not yet told her the story of the oak grove. For some reason she has been unable to talk about it.

'Weird,' says Georgy, when she hears about Megan's vocation. 'Really weird. I mean, it's a bit out of date, isn't it?'

Clarissa, however, is oddly defensive of Megan and Georgy backs off, intrigued. Now, as she silently enters Clarissa's bedroom, she remembers Clarissa's reluctance to discuss Megan and she decides that here is another little mystery to be teased out. She looks down at her friend's sleeping face, enjoying the power over her defencelessness, and prowls round the room on light feet. Clarissa is so heavily asleep that Georgy picks up the glass containing the remainder of the aunts' cordial and sniffs at it. Her eyebrows rise and her eyes widen; a smile lifts the corner of her mouth. There are so many little secrets to be discovered, so much to be attained, and she feels alert and alive as she goes out, gently closing the door behind her.

The work to prepare Thomas's quarters for his homecoming proceeds very slowly indeed. This is fortunate for everyone realises how difficult things will be when he returns home. Even Clarissa is beginning to regret her Florence Nightingale act to Matron; she wishes she has not been quite so brave and capable, so determined that she will help him to regain his strength.

'It's a pity,' says Georgy thoughtfully, 'that we can't tell them you're pregnant. There's no way a pregnant woman and two elderly ladies could cope with him. All that lifting and so on. They'd probably suggest that you wait until after you've had the baby.'

'But we *can't* tell him,' cries Clarissa for the millionth time. 'We've agreed that. We've gone over it and over it. It's bad luck that just before the accident Thomas and I weren't . . . Well, we weren't doing anything. And even if we had been there's still a gap. He might remember when we last . . . made love and then there would be trouble. We can't risk it.'

She looks appealingly at the aunts who nod their agreement. The risk is too great and they all know that Clarissa would not be able to bluff it out. If it were Georgy now . . .

'Thomas has a great deal of pride,' says Aunt Olwen. 'And he is not a fool.'

Clarissa slumps in the corner of the sofa. It seems odd to

be having these conversations with Thomas's aunts but she is beginning to give up caring about exposing her private life so publicly.

'In which case,' Georgy is saying, 'we must make certain that Thomas stays in hospital for a while. Until after the baby.'

Clarissa frowns. 'I don't see what difference it makes,' she protests. 'I can't suddenly spring the baby on him. For a start he'll see I'm pregnant fairly soon and even if he doesn't, how do I explain the baby when he comes home? "Oh, look, darling. I forgot to tell you I had a baby a couple of months ago. Slipped my mind completely. Welcome home!" It won't quite work, will it?'

'Not like that,' agrees Georgy. 'Obviously not. But I have a kind of idea.'

They look at her hopefully. Even the aunts are beginning to feel anxious, although they trust the Goddess implicitly. A way will be made clear and they are convinced that Georgy has been sent to them for a reason.

'Let's hear it,' says Clarissa wearily.

'I haven't really thought it through,' warns Georgy. 'But it goes something like this. Supposing it's me who's pregnant. Now, when Clarissa gets too big to hide it, supposing she goes off ostensibly to look after *me*. When it's all over we both come back here with the baby which Thomas thinks is mine. Then . . .'

She hesitates. The aunts remain silent but Clarissa is looking puzzled.

'How do you mean?' she asks. ' "Goes off"? Where would I go? And what happens about the baby? If Thomas thinks it's yours . . . ?'

She shakes her head, confused, and Georgy glances at the aunts. They watch her expressionlessly, waiting, and she senses the need for great caution.

'Look,' she says rapidly, 'the main concern is to keep the baby here. Am I right?'

'Yes,' say the aunts together immediately.

'Right,' says Georgy. 'Fine. Now the problem is how to get Thomas to accept it. We've more or less agreed that he will never believe that it is his child. OK. So what, then? Do we tell him that darling Clarissa's had a tiny slip and hope that he'll forgive her? According to you,' she looks at the aunts, 'he won't wear it and he'll give Clarissa and the baby the old heave-ho. So. What next? We conceal the fact that Clarissa is pregnant and tell him that the child is mine, hoping that at some point he is prepared to adopt the child as his own.'

Clarissa and the aunts stare at her.

'Why should he?' asks Clarissa, ignoring the other complications implicit in Georgy's plan. 'He's already got Megan. Why should he adopt your child?'

'I think,' says Aunt Olwen slowly, 'that he might be prevailed upon to take the child, especially if he thinks you are desperate to have a baby and he can no longer supply you with one. His sense of . . . guilt, I'm sure, might be . . .'

'Played on? Exploited?' suggests Georgy impatiently, when Aunt Olwen hesitates too long. 'Exactly. Also a baby will keep Clarissa at home and occupied. Otherwise she might seek entertainment elsewhere.'

There is a silence while everyone thinks this through.

'But why,' asks Clarissa slowly, 'wouldn't you want to keep your baby?'

Georgy looks at her, suppressing her irritation. 'Make a guess,' she says lightly. 'A) I'm not married. B) I've no money. How's that for starters?'

'But he thinks you *are* married,' argues Clarissa. 'I told him all about it.'

There is another silence. Georgy thinks quickly and wonders how she could have forgotten how very tiresome darling Clarissa can be.

'Look,' she says slowly and clearly, as though speaking to a mental defective, 'forget what actually is or isn't. This is simply a working scenario, a proposed *modus operandi*. Get it? Thomas won't care whether I'm divorced or living in a harem. He won't be interested. Right? With me so far? Good. So we tell him that I've been caught out. Nice girl gone wrong but I can't keep the baby. I can't afford a baby, I have to go out to work. It doesn't matter, for God's sake. The point is that there's a baby going spare and you want one. And I'm your oldest friend which is a point in it's favour. Yes? Still with me?'

The three of them nod and Georgy smiles and relaxes a little. Has she been a little too intense? She laughs, spreading out her hands and looking rueful.

'Sorry,' she says. 'Am I pushing in where I'm not wanted? You've only got to say. But I think that time's running out and Clarissa *is* my oldest dearest friend. Apart from Thomas noticing, Megan's going to guess something soon. It's lucky she was too preoccupied to notice anything amiss this last holiday but I suspect that she will at Christmas if we're not very careful. And she's going to mention it to Thomas.'

'Oh God,' cries Clarissa, frightened anew. 'But how can we *stop* her noticing? I shall be six months by Christmas.'

'We might just get away with it,' says Georgy slowly. 'Loose baggy clothes and perhaps you might not be too well. You've put on weight because of being in bed a lot and so on. Lucky she's so dreamy, I'm sure we'll scrape through somehow. I'll keep him distracted.'

'Will you be coming for Christmas?' asks Clarissa with genuine pleasure. 'Oh, that's great.'

Georgy bites her lip. She has overextended herself, nearly given herself away, and she is furious at her stupidity.

'Only if I'm needed,' she says brightly. 'It depends on what job I get, of course, but you must tell me if I'm needed.'

'Of *course* you'll be needed,' cries Clarissa.

Georgy smiles fondly at her whilst glancing quickly at the aunts who continue to remain silent and thoughtful. She feels nervous now, wondering how far they have seen, how much they guess.

'I'll do anything I can to help,' she says gently, with her sweetest smile, 'you know that.'

'But I still don't understand,' perseveres Clarissa, 'how we'd cope about actually having the baby. You say I'd go away to look after you, while in fact I'm having the baby. But where would I go?'

It is Aunt Olwen who answers the question.

'You wouldn't go anywhere, of course,' she answers quietly. 'You'd be here. No-one will know. No-one comes to the house. You'd be quite safe and in good hands. We'll look after you.'

To her surprise, Clarissa knows a moment of deep atavistic fear. Suddenly she longs for everything to be above board and legitimate. She wants to have her baby in a big bright hospital with a doctor and a midwife . . . and a registrar.

'What about birth certificates and things?' she asks.

The aunts are unconcerned about such legal niceties but Georgy sees her chance.

'This is why we must think it through carefully,' she says firmly, although she is trying to be far less intense. 'I have a feeling we may need to involve Evan.'

'Evan? But why?' wails Clarissa. 'Oh, I can't *stand* it.'

'It *is* his child,' points out Georgy calmly, 'and we might need his help. The baby will have to be officially registered. We certainly don't want to arouse suspicions but I'm sure I can deal with that side of it if only you will trust me.'

The aunts have lived too much in seclusion to see that this aspect of it might be difficult. They accept it, knowing that Evan knows many people and has many useful connections. Georgy wonders if it can be achieved without a great deal of questioning and is far less sanguine, nevertheless it has given them all something to think about. Only Clarissa remains unconvinced and frightened.

'I'd rather have it in hospital,' she says stubbornly. 'Supposing something goes wrong and we couldn't call a doctor? Oh dear. Perhaps I'd better tell Thomas the truth. I'm sure he'd forgive me if he knew how desperate I am and if necessary the baby will have to be adopted. Oh God! I really can't bear all this!' and she bursts into tears.

The aunts and Georgy exchange a glance and Georgy goes to sit beside Clarissa, to comfort her.

'Only wait,' she says persuasively. 'Only wait a little longer. Try to trust me. You've always trusted me, haven't you. Remember at school? And afterwards in London?'

Clarissa shifts uncomfortably, wiping her eyes, not wanting the aunts to know all the mistakes of her youth. She mumbles something and Georgy hugs her. Across Clarissa's head her eyes meet the level gaze of the aunts and she decides to test her power a little.

'You're quite safe,' she says to Clarissa. 'You have two wonderful guardians. They'll look after you when the time comes.'

Clarissa remembers the stab of fear that smote her when Aunt Olwen talked of her having the baby here at the house with no proper medical attention and she clings tightly to her really, *really* best friend.

'But you'll be here, too, won't you?' she asks. 'Can't you stay, Georgy? Please don't go. You can stay here with us, can't you?'

Above her head, Georgy looks at the aunts. She raises her eyebrows and pulls down her mouth almost comically. '*What now?*' she seems to be asking them. '*What on earth do I do now?*'

The aunts commune silently and it is Aunt Gwyneth who answers.

'Of course she must stay,' she answers. 'If she has no other commitments then we all hope she'll remain here with us for as long as she can put up with us.'

'There!' cries Clarissa, trying to smile a little now, feeling happier. 'You see? You can't go now.'

'Well then,' says Georgy, smiling back at her, 'you don't need to worry, do you? You know I'll look after you.'

'Are we right I wonder,' says Aunt Olwen later. She and Aunt Gwyneth are together in their sitting-room upstairs. 'I feel confused. Sometimes I think I'm getting too old to deal with what has to be done.'

'The Goddess will look after us,' replies Aunt Gwyneth after a moment or two. 'Georgy cannot have arrived at such a moment for no purpose. We were waiting for a Sign.'

'I feel anxious,' says Aunt Olwen. She picks up her knitting and puts it down again. She is restless and uneasy. 'You know I actually wondered whether . . . whether . . .'

'Yes?' prompts Aunt Gwyneth.

'The child,' says Aunt Olwen. 'We may die before the child is old enough to . . . help us and I actually found myself wondering whether Georgy . . .'

'She is a force,' agrees Aunt Gwyneth. 'She seems ready to . . . assist us without petty objections or mouthing moralities but . . .'

'It's early days,' says Aunt Olwen quickly.

'True,' nods Aunt Gwyneth. 'I think your intuition is right . . . but what might she want in return?'

Their eyes meet, full of fearful possibilities.

'We misjudged Clarissa,' murmurs Aunt Olwen. 'Her desires are not great enough. Not for Thomas nor for the house nor for Evan.'

'Nor even for the child,' Aunt Gwyneth reminds her.

Aunt Olwen groans. 'That is my fear,' she says softly. 'That we are getting too old to take correct judgments.'

'She is bearing the child. I feel its power even in the womb,' says Aunt Gwyneth. 'Remember Evan is descended from dear Mama, doubly a Mortimer. And he is quite ruthless. The child belongs to the Goddess.'

'I feel that, too,' admits Aunt Olwen. 'Yet I am fearful.'

'She will take what belongs to Her,' says Aunt Gwyneth confidently. 'But we need someone between us and the child. Someone who will act until the child is old enough to come into her inheritance.'

'Georgy?' whispers Aunt Olwen.

'Or Evan?' murmurs Aunt Gwyneth.

'Evan? *Here*?' asks Aunt Olwen. 'How? With Thomas and Clarissa . . . ?'

They lean close together and a cold current of air seems to pass between them, chilling the room. The wind comes from nowhere, howling round the chimneys, and the flames in the grate leap up high and die back as the two old women mutter together.

Downstairs in the small saloon Clarissa, dozing before the fire, wakes suddenly from a frightening dream and looks fearfully about her. She dreamed that the child was crying out in her womb, struggling to escape, and someone with bright, fierce eyes was bending over her. There is terror and menace in the room which is full of shadows and Clarissa sits quite still, wondering how many ghosts press about her, her heart thudding unevenly. She knows that the dead cannot hurt the living but when she tries to call out her voice scrapes in her throat and she is unable to move.

'He will come again with glory to judge both the quick and the dead whose kingdom shall have no end . . .' It is Megan's voice she hears and she looks round quickly, her fear receding, freed from the terrible paralysis of limb and voice. Of course, Megan is not there; she is far away at school. In fact, she is in chapel, this being Sunday evening, but Clarissa feels better now. She is able to get up and go out into the brightly-lit hall, into the drawing-room to pour herself a drink and wait for the others to join her.

As autumn draws on there is a period of calm. Georgy is afraid lest she has been too open, too eager, and she withdraws into the background a little. This is wise. Clarissa has begun to feel the least bit peevish; she is confused by her conflicting needs. She has pleasurably imagined how she was to be looking after poor old Georgy after all her ill-luck and how Georgy was to be grateful and humbled by the experience. Clarissa had it all planned. *She* was to be the good fairy, administering largesse, patronising her friend who had got it all wrong, but it hadn't worked out quite like that. To begin with Georgy had seemed envious of Clarissa's achievements, had been ready to congratulate and admire, but now their positions have been reversed. Clarissa has slipped back into her position of dependency and, although she is irritated, yet she cannot imagine managing just now without Georgy.

She reminds herself that she managed very well when Georgy went to America; that she has managed very well until very recently. If only it weren't for the baby . . . She says this to herself very rarely. The baby seems to take exception to it and retaliates by causing violent bouts of sickness; nevertheless, she wishes she could turn back the clock. She even feels she could have coped with Thomas, she could have cared for him and nursed him, and they could have been happy and peaceful together – if only it hadn't been for her one terrible lapse with Evan. Yet she would be miserable if Evan paid any attention to Georgy. She still thinks about him with as much love and longing as her lassitude will allow, although she sometimes wonders if she were bewitched by him, rather like Titania with Bottom.

It is when she thinks of the months ahead, of the concealment and the deceiving and the lying, that she feels weak with terror. Georgy's confidence and quick thinking are essential to her, so much so that Clarissa is too weak and idle to take her life back into her own hands and attempt to mould it to her own desires. Instead, she leaves it to Georgy and the aunts, preferring the easy option, prepared to suffer the frustration that goes with it. Once the baby is born and Thomas persuaded to adopt it, then she will take up the reins again . . . but how will she live without Evan?

Georgy, seeing Clarissa's confusion, decides to humour her so as to encourage a more submissive frame of mind. One blusterous October morning, knowing that Clarissa is idly reading a book in the small saloon, she brings her coffee and some of Aunt Olwen's excellent shortbread.

'I shall be as big as a house,' says Clarissa sulkily, refusing it – though with reluctance. She adores shortbread. 'I'm fed up with feeling so ill and worried all the time.'

'Poor darling,' coos Georgy gently. 'Poor old thing. How horrid this is for you. If it weren't for silly old Thomas life would be so simple, wouldn't it?'

'Would it?' Clarissa is momentarily surprised out of her sulks. She hasn't quite approached the problem from this angle. 'Why would it?'

Georgy bends over the cups so that Clarissa won't see that she is rolling her eyes in exasperation. She remembers that her really, *really* best friend was always a bear of little brain and it is best to use words of one syllable very slowly and loudly whilst introducing new ideas.

'Well,' she says lightly, 'he's the only person we have to worry about, isn't he?'

'It's the baby who's causing the problem,' retorts Clarissa crossly – poor old Thomas, honestly, it's a bit thick. 'If it weren't for the baby . . . aaargh!'

'Whatever is it?' cries Georgy, putting down the coffee pot and hurrying to Clarissa. 'Are you OK?'

'It's the baby.' Clarissa stares up at her, hands across her stomach. 'I think it moved. I felt a kind of . . . well . . . I think it *kicked* me.'

'How terrific,' cries Georgy excitedly. 'Honestly, darling. Imagine . . . Oh, you *are* lucky. Gosh, how I envy you.'

A little mollified by such enthusiasm and surprised by the energy of the baby, Clarissa allows herself to be persuaded to the shortbread.

'We have to look after you,' says Georgy solicitously, passing her a cup of coffee. 'So . . .' she sits beside her on the sofa. 'What were we saying? Oh yes, about poor old Thomas. If only he could have been a bit more . . . you know . . . active, you wouldn't have had to look elsewhere. He should have remembered that you're quite a bit younger than he is. You can't go marrying young pretty girls and expect them to behave like middle-aged women.'

'It's not really his fault,' says Clarissa staunchly – but she is not *quite* so ready to defend him now. He *was* neglectful, rather dreary and dull, now she thinks about it . . .

'And then he *would* go and fall off his tractor,' laughs Georgy, shaking her head reprovingly, as though he has done it quite wilfully so as to become a nuisance to his family on purpose. 'There must have been plenty of farm-hands or something to go about driving tractors.'

'Thomas liked to be in touch with his land,' says Clarissa – but the assurance has gone from her voice. It *was* careless of Thomas, he should have been more responsible.

'Never mind, darling,' says Georgy. 'Just think. When he dies you'll get all this.'

Clarissa stares at her. 'Dies?'

Georgy breathes deeply through her nose before beaming at her dear old friend. 'I know I'm looking ahead,' she says mendaciously, 'but he *is* quite a bit older than you are and then, you know, when you have that kind of accident, queer things often happen.'

'What kind of things?' Clarissa is riveted, her mouth hanging open.

Her hair is greasy, like wet string, and her skin is blotchy; not a pretty sight. Georgy surveys her dispassionately, wondering how she ever managed to trap not only Thomas but Evan, too.

'Oh all sorts of things,' she says evasively. 'It can affect the whole body, you see. It might be a stroke. Or a heart attack.'

'Oh God!' Clarissa is quite horrified by these revelations and Georgy sees that she has gone too far, too quickly. Clarissa needs to be more prepared for the idea.

'Sometimes,' she says sententiously, 'it can be kinder that way. Poor old Thomas. Imagine such an outdoor sort of chap confined to a wheelchair. Awful. No wonder he's always so depressed. I wonder how you'll manage when he comes home? Depressives can be so tricky to live with.'

'But don't you think he'll be happier when he gets home?' asks Clarissa anxiously.

Georgy purses her lips thoughtfully. 'Doubt it,' she says. 'It'll probably get worse. Imagine having to be confined to two rooms when you've had all this! You'll have your work cut out keeping him entertained. Poor old Clarissa. What rotten luck. And you'll have the baby to worry about, too.'

Clarissa is aghast at the picture that Georgy paints.

'The aunts will help,' she says. 'They can sit with Thomas and I shall look after the baby. Nan Ellis does most of the heavy work, after all.'

Georgy notices that she is not included in the future beyond the acceptance of the baby and her eyes narrow a little.

'You'll have to watch out for Nan Ellis, won't you?' she asks. 'If she notices you're pregnant everything will go up in smoke. She'll gossip and old Thomas will be on the scent . . .'

They both jump as Aunt Olwen speaks from behind them.

'Nan Ellis never gossips,' she says gently. 'She has seen what happens to people who speak out of turn. Her *nain* was struck dumb and paralysed for threatening to speak out of turn.'

The girls turn to stare up at her, even Georgy is silenced.

'What's a *nain*?' asks Clarissa faintly.

'It's Welsh for grandmother,' says Aunt Olwen. 'No, we have nothing to fear from Nan Ellis.'

She emphasises the name, as though there are others who should be watched, but Clarissa is too shocked to notice.

'But how?' she asks. 'What do you mean? Struck dumb?'

'You must remember that some parts of the countryside aren't quite so civilised as they appear on the surface,' Aunt Olwen tells her. 'Some of the old beliefs and superstitions are still very much alive. It would be foolish to under-rate them.'

'Do you mean,' asks the persistent Clarissa, 'that someone put a spell on her?'

'Some say that she was punished,' says Aunt Olwen carefully, 'for threatening to speak out of turn.'

Clarissa shivers. 'Gosh,' she says. 'That's really spooky. What was she going to speak about?'

'It's a long time ago,' says Aunt Olwen evasively, 'but Nan Ellis hasn't forgotten.'

Clarissa is silent, brooding on these bizarre happenings, but Georgy and Aunt Olwen stare at one another for a long moment and Georgy sees a warning in the cold, grey, bright eyes. She feels disquieted, almost fearful, and it is Georgy's eyes that drop before that older, fiercer gaze.

'It's funny, isn't it?' the unobservant Clarissa is saying. 'All these weird happenings. Ghosts and things and that funny place with the standing stones.'

'Standing stones?' asks Georgy, pulling herself together. She hasn't heard about the standing stones. 'What are you talking about?'

Clarissa comes to herself and looks around her. She feels a sensation of cold, as though something is warning her, and she wonders if one of the dear old ancestors has come in and is hovering about. She shivers, loses the thread of her thoughts – and feels the baby kick.

'Oooh!' she cries, clutching herself. 'Gosh, this baby is a real monster. Ooooooh!'

'Has the baby moved?' Aunt Olwen is round the sofa end in a flash, bending over the gasping Clarissa. She lays her hand on Clarissa's belly and feels the fluttering. The tremor moves up her arm and strikes into her heart and she cries out with delight, 'Already? How strong she is. Oh, this is a splendid moment.'

She fusses over Clarissa, pouring more coffee, calling for Aunt Gwyneth, and Georgy is momentarily ignored in all the fuss.

Georgy does not forget, however. She knows that she has had a warning but, away from the aunts, her confidence returns. They need her. She wonders what Clarissa meant about the standing stones and, at an opportune moment a day or two later, she announces that she is going for a walk. Evan is standing outside on the gravel smoking a cigarette, staring up at the house, his back to the drive.

'Had a visitor?' asks Georgy, watching a small car vanishing out of the gate and realising that she's seen it before.

'My daughter came to see me,' answers Evan easily.

'Nice,' says Georgy. 'Very devoted. Close family are you?'

Evan laughs. Georgy amuses him with her manipulations and deviousness but he is unaffected by her.

'I'm an unfaithful, lying bastard,' he says genially. 'My wife seeks consolation in the arms of an old, loyal boyfriend. My son hates me for it and left home as soon as he could. My daughter continues to love me for reasons unknown to me. Mainly, I suspect, because she and her ma fight like cats.'

'Well,' says Georgy admiringly. 'That's a pretty succinct answer. A nice little word-picture of the happy home. I expect you're really pissed-off with the set-up here?'

He watches her thoughtfully, smiling a little. 'Why should I be?'

Georgy shrugs. 'Must be tough watching old Thomas inheriting all this. And now your child will be lording it here and you can't even acknowledge it.'

'What would you suggest?' he asks, still smiling.

'Oh, lots of things,' she says lightly. 'Where shall I start? Tell Thomas the truth and insist on a cut of the estate to keep you quiet? Murder Thomas, marry Clarissa and live here with your child? Murder both of them, having first blackmailed them into making their wills in your favour? . . . Shall I go on?'

'Sounds quite enough for a start,' he answers.

She laughs to let him see that it is all a joke but he doesn't laugh with her and she becomes more sober.

'I think it's terrific,' she tells him earnestly, 'that you've let yourself be used in this whole business. It's really generous to do all this and then be prepared to stand back and be forgotten. Not at all the behaviour of – how did you describe yourself? – an unfaithful, lying bastard. More like a dear old pussycat. Still, those old aunts of yours are powerful women.' She chuckles suddenly. 'Funny isn't it, how wrong one can be? *They* look like pussycats and are as tough as old boots, whereas *you* . . .'

She breaks off and beams at him.

'Appearances,' he says softly, 'can be deceptive.'

She looks at him, one eyebrow raised provocatively.

'I've heard that, too,' she says. 'Well, must be off. I'm going for a walk. So where are these famous standing stones, then?'

His expression changes and she watches him, surprised at the sudden difference and faintly unnerved.

'I'd stay away from the grove,' he says. 'I really would. Not a good place for a walk. I should stick to the lanes and the fields if I were you.'

'But you, my dear Evan, are not me,' says Georgy, recovering herself. '*I* am not scared by ghosties and ghoulies and things that go bump in the night.'

She turns away into the trees and he watches her go, his expression grim. She follows the path until it peters out and the trees crowd closer but still she is drawn forward. The stones, when she comes upon them, take her rather by surprise placed as they are in the wide clearing. She wanders into the bright circle, touching the rough, pitted surfaces, but her attention is drawn to the darkness beyond. This is a darkness which is deeper than the shadows and, despite herself, her heart speeds a little as she strains her eyes to see what lies beneath those ancient boughs; humps of earth, like graves, and things lying on a flat rectangular slab, things that gleam ghostly white, like picked bones . . .

The light touch on her shoulder brings her round, gasping, and Evan smiles down at her.

'So you found them,' he says. 'And what do you think of our own private little Stonehenge?'

'Not a lot,' she says, recovering herself quickly. Damned if she is going to lose face in front of Evan. She looks up at him and feels a tug of attraction. He is so tall and fair and his smile is . . .

'I've been thinking about what you were saying earlier,' he

is saying. 'It occurs to me that you have a certain interest here yourself. Or why are you letting yourself be used, too?'

They have moved out of the circle, back towards the path, and Georgy's spirits are rising.

'Oh, I'm doing it for love,' she says carelessly. 'Poor, darling Clarissa needs me to get her out of the shit.'

'And afterwards?' he asks.

She shrugs, aware of his hand gripping her arm.

'Got any suggestions?' she asks mockingly.

'Yes,' says Evan. 'I think I have.'

Allhallows Even: the ancient pagan festival of the dead. The aunts are busy; eyes bright, lips pressed into secret smiles, they bustle about. As the day draws on, the wind keens about the house and the trees bow before its passing. The flames burn orange and red and tall shadows billow out of corners and dance across ceilings; branches tap at darkening windows and the wooden timbering creaks and groans.

Clarissa turns on all the lights in the drawing-room after dinner and huddles in a chair by the fire. For some reason she has avoided the small saloon all day and she is pleased to see Georgy who has been rather elusive since teatime.

'I hate the wind,' she complains, pulling one of the aunts' shawls more closely round her shoulders. 'It sounds like a child weeping.'

'Hallowe'en,' says Georgy with relish, perching on the brass fender. 'Witches on broomsticks and things. Isn't it supposed to be when the dead walk or something?'

'So what's different about tonight?' asks Clarissa with a rare flash of humour. 'They do it all the time in this house.'

'You don't really believe that!' exclaims Georgy scathingly. 'What a load of balls. Honestly. Megan was pulling your leg.'

'I don't think she was,' protests Clarissa. 'Sometimes I think I feel them myself.'

Georgy raises her eyebrows scornfully; darling Clarissa always was so suggestible, always ready to believe that men were dying of love for her or that her girlfriends hated her. It was just a case of clever words at the right moment. She hasn't changed a bit. Georgy yawns elaborately to indicate her boredom and Clarissa feels slightly foolish.

'I've been thinking,' she says. 'Won't your parents be wondering what's happened to you? They don't know you're here, do they?'

Georgy looks at her sharply. Is there something hidden behind the casual question?

'They think I'm having a holiday in Canada,' she says carelessly. 'A friend of mine was going on a long tour so I wrote some letters to be posted along the way. She's going to put some appropriate postcards in with them.'

Clarissa laughs delightedly. 'Honestly,' she says admiringly. 'You certainly think of everything, don't you? But you'll have to tell them sometime, won't you?'

'All in good time,' says Georgy easily. 'They'll only whinge on.'

'Even so,' says Clarissa, with her irritating habit of worrying a subject to death, 'they can't think you've been on holiday this long.'

'No,' says Georgy after a moment, 'no, they can't, can they?'

The truth of the matter is that Georgy has had a violent falling out with her parents over certain matters concerning borrowing money under false pretences and lying of a very grave nature. She was never married to the American with whom she had an affair and has lost her job because she was too over-confident and made one or two serious mistakes. The abortion – Clarissa thinks she had a miscarriage – was the last straw. She cannot bear the thought of her friends or family knowing about her failure: especially not her family. There has been a complete breakdown between them for some considerable time and Georgy doesn't care if communication is never resumed.

'You can always phone them from here if you want to,' says Clarissa, made generous at the remembrance of poor Georgy's misfortunes. 'I'm sure they'll understand, Georgy. You've had such a rough ride but it'll pass. Time is a great healer.'

'Talking of which,' says Georgy, suppressing the urge to bat Clarissa over her smug head with the long-handled, iron chestnut toaster, 'we mustn't forget that the clocks go back tonight at midnight. That's the witching hour. Wonder if you'll see your spirits walk?'

'She certainly will not,' announces Aunt Gwyneth, bustling in. 'She needs her sleep. We'll all have a nice early night, shall we?'

'I hate early nights,' says Georgy, stabbing at the fire with short jabs of the poker. 'I shall never sleep with this wind howling round the house.'

'It's turning cold,' says Aunt Olwen, appearing suddenly. 'I thought we might have a warming nightcap.'

Georgy sits up straight, senses alert. 'Good idea,' she says cheerfully, 'that was a delicious wine we had with dinner. Lovely fruity taste.'

She watches keenly as Aunt Olwen fiddles about at the drinks tray, her back to them all, and she takes her glass meekly enough, swirling the liquid thoughtfully.

'One of my own little receipts,' says Aunt Olwen proudly. 'Now, no gulping. Try to savour it. Can anyone tell me what's in it?'

Georgy thinks it's extremely unlikely that she or Clarissa will be able to guess anything of the kind but Clarissa, who is sipping eagerly, hazards one or two ideas.

'Blackcurrant?' she cries. 'Raspberry?'

Georgy takes a sip and allows the liquid to stream gently back through her teeth into the glass.

'Poppy juice?' she suggests idly and laughs to show that she is jesting.

The aunts look at her reprovingly. Clarissa laughs too, swallows some of the cordial down the wrong way, and has a choking fit. The aunts put down their glasses and hurry to help her. Unhurriedly, Georgy leans forward and empties the contents of her glass at the very back of the fire; slowly she stretches out to pick up a log and throws it onto the flames so that the fire sparks and blazes up.

'Terrific,' she says, when the fuss has died down and Clarissa is wiping her streaming eyes. 'Absolutely yummy.'

She licks her lips appreciatively and the aunts beam at her. Oddly, after a bit, she does begin to feel rather drowsy, warm and sleepy, and she moves further away from the fire. Clarissa is dozing in her chair and the aunts give tiny yawns from time to time. Presently they all decide to go to bed. Georgy does not undress, however. She opens the window so that the cold air beats upon her face and then sits down on the edge of the bed. Her eyes are heavy with sleep but she keeps them fixed on her watch.

The distant light from flickering lamps guide her through the darkness. Twigs pull at her clothes, whipping sharply against her cheeks, and a thousand voices are carried shrieking through the turbulent air. Shivering, she stumbles from the path into the trees whose topmost branches thrash in the wind, drawn ever forward by the gleam of lights between the black bare boles. Some winged creature – bat or owl? – swoops past and she gasps, ducking away. It dives again and for a brief moment she sees the cruel hooked beak, the huge yellow eyes, and beats out at it wildly. A few yards more and she reaches the open grassy space. She dares not go too close but stands within the stone circle, straining her eyes to see into the grove beyond. Two dark, hooded shapes mop and mow before the slab, arms are raised over some small animal and there is a single scream, suddenly cut off, which causes her to stifle a cry of horror.

There is a more violent gust of wind and she is aware of a powerful and terrifying presence hovering close to her, pressing down upon her. She turns to run and crashes into something solid; something warm and strong. Her scream is muffled, she feels she is being suffocated, and her knees buckle as she sinks into unconsciousness.

She wakes at last, senses still swimming, the nightmare fading. Abruptly she sits up, remembering now, and stares about her in the broad daylight. She is on the top of her bed, fully dressed, and the window is still open; a steady rain drums on the glass and soaks the window seat. She sits motionless, thinking. Presently she draws up her knees and examines her shoes. They are dry, free of earth or leaf. She frowns, recalling how drowsy she was last night, how hard it was to keep her eyes open as she sat on her bed, waiting for midnight. She has a bitter taste in her mouth and her head aches painfully. Was her visit to the grove simply a dream? But why should she sleep so heavily and dream so vividly? After all, she didn't drink the cordial . . . In a flash of illumination, she remembers the wine at dinner. '*Lovely fruity taste*' she'd said.

Despite herself, she chuckles, wondering what they slipped into her wine that resulted in such an hallucinogenic effect. It is clear that they do not trust her – yet. She re-examines her dream, trying to recall the sensations of menace and terror. Did she actually hear the scream as she lay in a stupor upon her bed or was it part of the dream? She has no doubt that the two old aunts have been up to some superstitious nonsense in the grove – she'd been watching and waiting all yesterday for some sign of it – but surely not *sacrifice*? She remembers the humps of earth and the white gleaming shapes on the slab and frowns. '*Some of the old beliefs and superstitions are very much alive. It would be foolish to under-rate them.'* Someone has said that very recently . . .

Georgy slips off the bed and goes to shut the window. The room is very cold and she stands still, hugging herself, rubbing her hands up and down her arms, deep in thought. She is beginning to realise that there is much more here than is at first apparent. She has simply assumed that the two dotty old aunts are determined to get an heir for their beloved house before they die and are prepared to go to any lengths to achieve it. She has no doubt that they connived at Clarissa's affair with Evan, once it was clear that Thomas would be fathering no more children, and that they have welcomed *her* so readily because she is a means of introducing the child to Thomas. It is evident that they occasionally drug Clarissa so as to keep her reasonable – but where exactly does the grove come into all this? There are undercurrents she simply does not understand and she is cross that they duped her yesterday when she might have learned more.

She glances at her watch and stands quite still with shock. It is after midday. Her first reaction is one of anger that she has been put out of action so efficiently; the second is one of admiration. They may be as mad as March hares but there are certainly no flies on the dear old aunts. They must take their antics in the grove very seriously indeed. Georgy, who is determined to have a future here in this wonderful house, wonders how she can convince them that she is on their side – whatever that might entail.

They are waiting for her when she comes downstairs. They watch her slyly as she appears in the kitchen where they are preparing lunch but make no attempt to speak, apart from the usual greeting.

'I know it's nearly lunch time,' she says, 'but do you mind if I make some coffee? I have *the* most frightful headache.'

Making sympathetic noises they make room for her,

murmuring gently, moving a pan of soup, fetching her a cup and saucer. As she looks at them, she cannot seriously believe that they are truly a threat – or, at least, only as the mad are a threat. She laughs suddenly.

'*Only the mad*,' she says to herself. '*Only . . .*'

They look at her enquiringly and she shakes her head.

'Just remembering the dream I had last night,' she explains. 'Well, more like a nightmare, really.' She knows that she dare not give in to them, so she smiles provocatively. 'I don't know what you put in that drink last night but I had quite a trip.'

They shoot out their lips consideringly, looking knowing and wise.

'Of course if you're not used to home-made cordial,' they say, 'it can have rather a strange effect . . .'

'You're not wrong,' she agrees, 'but I wasn't talking about the cordial.'

They look at her out of the corners of their eyes, still smiling slyly, saying nothing, and Georgy cannot help but laugh. They look like two naughty old pussycats.

'You're wicked,' she says, 'but I'll let you off this time. Just this once.'

She takes her coffee and goes off to find Clarissa. A small silence is left behind her.

'She believes it to be a dream,' says Aunt Olwen, after a moment.

'It would seem so,' agrees Aunt Gwyneth. 'She must have a very strong head.'

'It is certainly as well that Evan warned us,' says Aunt Olwen. 'He feared that he might have harmed her but she looks perfectly recovered.'

'We must be very careful,' warns Aunt Gwyneth. 'She was an alien presence in the grove. Not welcomed.'

'She is not what we hoped for but she is useful,' murmurs Aunt Olwen thoughtfully. 'We need her for the time being.'

'And then?' whispers Aunt Gwyneth. 'I suspect that she will not leave readily.'

Their eyes meet, cold, ruthless, calculating.

'Is lunch nearly ready?' asks Clarissa, coming in behind them. 'I'm starving. Gosh, it's so *chilly* in here. It's usually so cosy.'

'Nice hot soup to start with,' says Aunt Olwen briskly. 'All ready. And warm rolls fresh out of the oven. Off you go, into the dining-room. Here. Take these plates.'

'Georgy's got the most frightful head,' says Clarissa, hovering. 'Have we got any aspirin?'

'Poor Georgy,' say the aunts. 'Perhaps she drank a drop too much wine last night. Never mind. An aspirin will soon put her right. Two perhaps. Here you are. She can put her feet up in the small saloon after lunch.'

'Megan's home on Thursday for half-term,' says Clarissa cheerfully. 'We'll have to think of something to do for her.'

'I expect she'll be wanting to visit her father,' says Aunt Olwen. 'We'll take her in.'

'I'll come, too,' says Clarissa. 'I shan't be able to visit for much longer so I must make the most of it while I can. Oh dear. I'm going to find it so hard to lie to Thomas.'

'We shall be with you,' say the aunts encouragingly. 'You know that you are quite safe with us.'

'Honestly,' says Clarissa, going into the dining-room where Georgy sits, elbows on table, head in hands. 'They are just *so* sweet, aren't they?'

'Absolute poppets,' says Georgy drily, trying not to move her head.

'Here are the aspirin,' says Clarissa, her mind still on the aunts. 'Take them with your coffee. They are so *totally* reliable. They've taken this baby thing so well. I thought they'd throw me out. Wherever would I be without them?'

The answer to this is quite simple. Clarissa would be safely in her flat in Fulham, with no crippled husband, no haunted house, no mad aunts and no illegitimate child, but Georgy resists the temptation to tell her so. Lunch arrives in time to provide a distraction and the moment passes.

13

Georgy's affair with Evan starts almost casually. Megan's imminent arrival lends the house an air of normality: special cooking to be done, her room aired and bed made up. The aunts encourage the two girls to drive into the town to visit Thomas whilst all this is being done. It has been agreed that Georgy should not meet Thomas yet – 'We shall have to stuff a pillow down your front' giggles Clarissa – but she has an idea of how she might fill in the time while Clarissa is visiting. The aunts make it easy for her to implement her plan. They suggest that she could just pop in to see Evan to find out when he might be coming to continue the alterations. They have not seen him for several days and dislike leaving messages on his answerphone. Georgy maintains an air of indifference to this request but promises that she will look in at his office. They set off quite soon after breakfast, Clarissa twittering nervously.

'Do you think he'll notice?' she asks for the fiftieth time.

'No,' says Georgy, who hates being driven and is wondering when someone might suggest that the car should be insured for her to drive. 'Lucky that you've always been chubby. It hardly shows at all. Specially in that night-gown effort.'

Clarissa is offended by the description both of her shape and her garment.

'At least I've *got* a figure,' she says spitefully. 'No-one could mistake *me* for a boy.'

'That's true,' agrees Georgy rather too readily.

Clarissa changes gear crossly and Georgy pulls herself together; no point in alienating her meal ticket to the future.

'I'm really upset that I can't meet Thomas,' she says, infusing a kind of wistful fretfulness into the statement. 'I wonder if perhaps I've been a bit harsh on him. In the early days you made him sound rather a sweetie.'

Clarissa is silent. It is thus that Georgy keeps her off balance. Clarissa has just managed to convince herself that Thomas is thoughtless, middle-aged and rather dull. Now Georgy is implying that she might have got it wrong. Clarissa finds that she is tempted to encourage this latter idea, to sing Thomas's praises, thereby winning Georgy's envy, but she is confused and therefore says nothing at all. They are passing the spot where Aunt Olwen unseated the cyclist and Clarissa recounts the story to Georgy, adding the joke about the two types of pedestrians being the quick and the dead. Georgy laughs immoderately and Clarissa feels clever.

'I've always enjoyed that joke,' says Georgy. 'I was about six when I heard it the first time. Of course neither of those old dears should be driving at all. Well past their sell-by date, I fear.'

'Oh, come on,' says Clarissa, diverted from the irritation caused by the first part of Georgy's remark by the fear engendered by the second. 'They're pretty good for their ages.'

'Hmm,' murmurs Georgy doubtfully. 'But how much longer can they keep it up? With you and Thomas and a baby to look after they'll certainly have their work cut out.'

'I shall be OK as soon as I've had the baby,' protests Clarissa, resenting being lumped in with the weak and helpless. 'It's only the pregnancy that's making me feel rotten. We shall manage somehow.'

Georgy makes several little faces which imply doubt, pity

and resignation, all of which Clarissa sees out of the corner of her eye.

'Perhaps you can get Nan Ellis in a bit more,' suggests Georgy. 'You'll certainly need to when the aunts pop off. It's a big house. And then you'll really have your hands full with Thomas and a child. Those old biddies do more than you think. You'll really miss them when they go.'

'Oh don't talk about dying,' shivers Clarissa. 'I can't bear to think of it.'

'You have to look ahead,' says Georgy. 'Be prepared. Perhaps you could get a housekeeper. You'll be a bit lonely once the old dears . . . aren't with you any more. You'll need someone to have a bit of a laugh with. Someone your own age. Know what I mean? Is that the hospital? You'd better not drop me too close just in case someone sees me. There might be some nosey person who will recognise me later on and remember that I wasn't pregnant at the appropriate moment.'

'I'll drop you nearer into the town centre,' says Clarissa. 'Then I can show you the wine bar where we'll meet later. I hope you won't be too bored.'

Georgy strolls down the High Street feeling on top form. Really Clarissa is just too easy to manipulate to derive any great satisfaction from their little tussles but she has enjoyed wrong-footing her and putting doubts in her mind, as well as planting a seed or two. She does not hurry to Evan's office but pauses to look in a few shop windows and even wonders whether to have a cup of coffee. She decides against it, guessing that Evan will offer her one, assuming that he is there.

Evan is waiting for her, although he gives no sign of it. The aunts have already telephoned to tell him that she is on her way. He rises lazily from his desk and sketches a little bow.

'To what do I owe this pleasure?' he murmurs, setting a chair for her. 'No dramas, I hope?'

'Only the usual kind,' answers Georgy. She is aware of a little fizz of chemistry between them and her spirits rise still higher. 'The aunts are getting anxious. They haven't seen you for a while and they wonder when you might be coming to get on with some work.'

She deliberately phrases it in a faintly insulting way, implying that he is merely a workman, but he grins as he sits down again. He is remembering his last visit to the aunts – and his last encounter with Georgy – and he feels a sense of power, knowing that she has no idea of what has happened in the grove.

'Been missing me, have you?' he asks provocatively.

'I don't know about them,' she answers indifferently, 'but *I* have. Three women, two elderly and one pregnant, aren't my idea of stimulating company.'

He laughs at her, enjoying her direct approach, knowing that he must keep one step ahead.

'How *is* Clarissa?' he asks with genuine solicitousness.

Georgy shrugs. 'OK. Pregnancy has made her dull. She was always lazy but mentally she's not as sharp as she used to be. She's not quite so ready to have a bit of fun but I expect she'll be back to normal after the baby is born.'

'Don't be so sure of it,' warns Evan. 'My wife changed completely after the babies came. Mad for me she was, to begin with, but once she'd had the babies she took against me. Burst into tears every time she saw me.'

'I expect the scales dropped from her eyes,' says Georgy. 'Clever old Mother Nature fooled her for just as long as it took to propagate the species and then she suddenly saw you for what you are.'

'And what's that?' asks Evan, amused.

'An unfaithful, lying bastard,' quotes Georgy, beaming at

him. 'I expect it came as a bit of a shock to her. Do I get a cup of coffee?'

'Smacked bottom, more like,' he answers.

'Sounds like fun,' she says casually. 'Man of all trades, aren't you?'

'And master of all,' he replies. 'Just in case you're wondering. Come through to the flat and talk to me while I boil the kettle.'

Clarissa isn't having nearly so much fun. As she approaches Thomas's ward, the matron appears and draws her into her office.

'We have some really good news for you,' she tells the nervous Clarissa. 'Your husband has made some new progress in the last few days and we'd like to send him to a London clinic which deals with his kind of problems. We can't promise but we're very hopeful that he might become more mobile.'

'Do you mean,' asks Clarissa, 'that he might walk again?'

'Now that's much too premature,' chides Matron gently. 'I know how determined you are but we must take it one step at a time.' She laughs at her little joke and pats Clarissa's arm. 'He'll be gone for a few weeks but I'm sure we'll see a great improvement when he returns. I'm quite confident that he'll be able to come home to you by Christmas.'

'By Christmas?' gasps Clarissa in horror. She pulls herself together and grins manically at Matron. 'By *Christmas*!' she carols in well-simulated delight. 'Oh, I can hardly believe it.'

'I knew you'd be thrilled,' says Matron. 'We know how much it means to you to have him home and to be encouraging him and helping him. I can't tell you how hard we've all worked. He's a great favourite with us now, you know, and that's thanks to you, my dear. You've been a brick.'

Clarissa stares at Matron, who is beaming with self-satisfaction, and remains struck dumb with panic. If only

Georgy or the aunts were with her they would be able to deal with this unforeseen happening. Matron takes her silence for a wordless joy and is deeply touched.

'I do hope,' says Clarissa, suddenly inspired, 'that we shall have the alterations done in time. It would be impossible as things are at the moment and the builder is so . . . so unreliable.'

'I'm quite sure that you'll both be equal to a few little difficulties,' says Matron archly, seeing Clarissa's anxiety as mere wifely concern for Thomas's well-being. 'You have six weeks to get your builder organised. Much can be achieved in six weeks with your kind of determination. I'm glad to see you looking so well. Put on a little weight, I think? It suits you. Now, come and see him. He's been longing to see you so as to tell you the news. The telephone is so unsatisfactory in these situations, isn't it? The dear man is so excited at the thought of this trip to London. I know I can count on you to be positive.'

'Preacher's dog's gone missing,' says Nan Ellis, puffing and panting as she makes Megan's bed. 'Just before Hallowe'en. Put notices up everywhere, he has. Nasty smelly old thing.'

'You shouldn't speak like that about Reverend Pauley,' says Aunt Olwen reprovingly, tucking sheets neatly, hospital corners. 'He's not as young as he was, no doubt.'

Nan emits a dry honking sound, something between shock and laughter. 'Not *preacher*,' she exclaims. 'The dog. Always round the dustbins. No bitch on heat is safe unless it's locked in a room with no door and no windows. Terrible mangy thing.'

'I'm surprised he misses it,' murmurs Aunt Olwen. 'Have I seen it, I wonder?'

'Welsh collie,' says Nan. 'White with one blue eye. Cunning thing. No loyalty. Go off with anyone for a biscuit. Should've been put down years ago. Went for a little boy a few months past but being preacher's dog it was all hushed up.'

'Perhaps,' suggests Aunt Olwen, 'perhaps someone has taken the law into his – or her – own hands?'

'Might've,' says Nan. 'Wouldn't blame 'em.'

'Rough justice,' says Aunt Olwen. 'That is what it is called, I believe. I think I'll find an extra rug. The nights are so cold . . .'

'But what shall we *do*?' twitters Clarissa. 'We *can't* have him home for Christmas. Oh *God* . . .'

Georgy forks up some fettucini. The morning has produced plenty of novelty and she is rather excited by these new developments. Evan has proved a stimulating companion and she has enjoyed an active and invigorating hour or two in his flat. Now there is the news that Thomas will be home for Christmas. After her physical exercise she is ready to stretch her mental capacity.

'You don't seem very concerned,' says Clarissa crossly, finishing her savoury pancake – terror always makes her hungry – and buttering another piece of roll. 'If Thomas comes home, we'll both have to go away somewhere.'

'Stop panicking,' says Georgy easily. 'We'll think of something.'

Clarissa looks at her suspiciously. She feels that Georgy is taking the news far too calmly. Also there is a sleek, contented look about her which is new . . .

'Why were you so late?' asks Clarissa sharply. 'Where did you go whilst I was with Thomas?' A horrid thought assails her. 'Did you see Evan?'

'Evan?' asks Georgy casually. 'Oh, Evan. Yes, I dropped in to see him. He was rather busy but he says he'll be out at the house tomorrow.'

Clarissa is lulled by Georgy's indifference, too preoccupied with this new problem to pursue her suspicions further.

'It's all very well,' she says peevishly, 'to say "stop panicking". It's all right for you. You can just pack up and leave whenever you feel like it.'

Georgy glances at her sharply. Does she really believe this to be the case? Perhaps she has gone a little too far, has been a touch over-confident.

'I can't afford to let you get in a state,' she says in a caressing voice. 'I'm here to look after you, you know that. You must leave it all to me. I'll deal. Remember that even if he does come home, Thomas will be confined to his quarters. He needn't see me at all and we'll pretend that you have a virulent strain of flu or something. It's no good looking too far ahead. This is one day at a time stuff. Between us all we'll cope.'

Clarissa, ever ready to be convinced, looks a little happier. Georgy watches her and thinks about all the things that Evan has said to her earlier. There is much to brood upon and she is surprised and delighted by Evan's breadth of vision.

'I suppose you're right,' says Clarissa, finishing her bread.

'Of course I'm right,' says Georgy bracingly. 'Now, how about some of the lemon drizzle. I'm sure you could manage a helping . . .'

14

As Evan goes about his work – opening up a long-concealed connecting door, building ramps, converting an old scullery into a specially designed shower and bathroom – his mind is occupied with his private thoughts. It seems that long-nurtured dreams might well come to fruition. To be in the house of his ancestors gives him a deep satisfaction and his ambitions grow stronger, the rewards more desirable. He studies the women of the house as he defines and re-defines his plans. His aunts he knows of old, ever since he was a little boy and brought to see his grandmother, their formidable mother. Not that the relationship was formally recognised but his mother, another strong-willed woman, eventually told him the truth. Even when he was small, the house fascinated him, drawing him back, enveloping him with its promise. Once Thomas inherited, Evan's visits became infrequent but he has always retained contact with his aunts. Even they, however, have no idea of the extent of his ambition.

He is aware of Georgy as he passes to and fro. He thinks of their morning together in his flat and smiles to himself. He sees that she is as ruthless as he is and realises that they make a powerful team. Evan is in a strong position: he has the confidence of the aunts but he sees a way, as yet unknown to them, that he might advance his own cause through Georgy.

There are several routes now open to him and he considers each of them very carefully. He has a surprisingly unswerving sense of family – Mortimer family – and he is prepared to wait – has he not waited all these years? – and to pursue each option thoroughly. He is determined that the succession of his house shall be secured, whatever sacrifice might be necessary. Georgy must be held in reserve; her desire for the house is a useful weapon in his armoury.

When he sees Clarissa he is kind to her. Now that her shame has been diluted into other more acceptable emotions she is able to respond to him, although with a certain amount of caution. He finds this challenging and his interest in her quickens again. He remembers how he enjoyed those few encounters with her and he exerts his charm. It pleases him to see how readily she responds and how jealousy begins to ferment between the two girls. Clarissa has the merit of being the mother of his child and is due a certain amount of consideration which Georgy clearly resents – and fears. Georgy, however, is thin, vital, attractive, clever and available, which Clarissa clearly envies – and fears.

The child is the catalyst. The whole household thinks of little else. Evan wonders if the other women realise what a weapon they are handing Georgy in agreeing that she shall be the means of bringing it into the family; that it is to be, as far as Thomas is concerned, *her* child. As far as he can tell, Clarissa simply doesn't think at all and his aunts' faith is placed immovably in the Goddess. Evan has a healthy atavistic respect for things he does not understand, he does not believe that puny man's knowledge has yet encompassed all things in this vast universe, but at the same time he also accepts that a genetic brew is passed down from generation to generation and he wonders exactly what kind of child he and Clarissa have made. He thinks about Thomas, wondering how he will react, and he also considers the rival merits of a quick Thomas and a dead Thomas.

Of Megan he does not think at all, thinking her to be safely out of the frame, her feet far advanced on the road to the convent. Yet when he meets her again for the first time for many, many years, he has a shock. She comes upon him suddenly at the turning of a passage and he experiences a real sense of disquiet. She stands quite still, her eyes wide and blank, as if they are looking at something else just beyond him, and he feels the hair rising on his neck. It is as if, in that moment, all his plans are spread before those far-seeing eyes.

'Megan,' he says loudly, as if determined to break the spell which encircles them. 'You must be Megan. The last time I saw you, you were a just a little girl.'

'You are Evan.' It is a statement, as if she is getting something clear in her own mind, and she frowns a little.

'Yes,' he says quickly. He guesses now that her gift is neither well-developed nor much used, her religious training will have held it in abeyance no doubt, and he needs to confuse her. 'That's quite right. I'm working on the alterations so that your father can come home as soon as possible. It's good news, isn't it, that he's going to a London clinic?'

'Good news,' she repeats slowly, still frowning. 'Yes. Yes, it is . . .'

'Come,' he says, taking her by the arm. 'Come and see what I've done. It's difficult, you know, in such an old house. So many steps and corners . . .'

He goes on talking and she allows herself to be led along the passage, to be shown what has been done for her father's comfort. Presently, when he runs out of words, the silence is huge and echoing.

'You are my kinsman,' she says courteously, as though she is continuing an earlier conversation.

'Yes,' says Evan – and sighs. He has been wasting his time. 'I am a kind of cousin, several times removed.'

'I had a strange feeling when I first saw you,' she begins,

pauses, shakes her head. 'I saw a woman standing close behind you,' she breathes. 'A woman with fierce, bright eyes who does not belong here. Not yet. She was not one of the Silent Ones and yet I felt I knew her.'

Evan feels a chill along his bare forearms and his tongue is cloven to the roof of his mouth. For some reason this gentle certainty unnerves him more than some of the more violent and terrifying things he has seen in the grove and he swallows, his eyes locked with hers . . .

'So *there* you are,' cries Aunt Olwen cheerfully. 'I was just thinking that it might be time for some coffee. You'd like some? You would? Good. Good. Come along Megan, my dear. Yours is already in the small saloon. You'll find Clarissa and Georgy will have eaten all the shortbread if you don't hurry up.'

'You should have warned me,' says Evan grimly, once Megan has disappeared. 'I thought you said we needn't worry about Megan.'

Aunt Olwen clicks her tongue distressfully and pats his shoulder encouragingly. 'She has the Sight,' she says. 'You know that. It's nothing more . . .'

'Nothing *more*?' cries Evan, who is frightened and cross with himself for still feeling shaken by the encounter. 'She's *dangerous*.'

'Nonsense,' says Aunt Olwen calmly. 'The church discourages such things and Megan is merely a beginner. She sees the ghosts, of course, but so do we all.'

'Do we?' asks Evan with a touch of sarcasm. 'Are you sure?'

'Don't you?' counters Aunt Olwen – and Evan is silent for a moment.

'I can feel them,' he mutters at last. 'And occasionally I see . . . something. The flick of a skirt. A movement in the shadows.'

'You haven't had the practice,' says Aunt Olwen comfortably. 'It will come. Megan was brought up with it, you see.

Sometimes she is a little awkward to have about but you mustn't overrate her abilities.'

'That's all right then,' says Evan rather tartly, recovering himself somewhat. 'I feel much better now.'

Aunt Olwen laughs at him, shaking her head reprovingly. 'My dear boy,' she says, 'you're a little overwrought. I shall get you some coffee straightaway.'

Evan watches her go and takes a deep breath, hoping that he has not made a mistake. In future he will be more careful.

'What did he mean by the word "dangerous"?' whispers Aunt Gwyneth. 'In what way can Megan be dangerous to us?'

'She might see too much,' mutters Aunt Olwen.

'Her gift is under-developed. She would never let us use her when she was a child,' murmurs Aunt Gwyneth. 'And the nuns have seen that it has remained dormant, although occasionally it gets the better of her.'

'Perhaps she saw something Evan would rather she did not see,' suggests Aunt Olwen. 'Something he is keeping from us . . .'

Their eyes meet, calculating, devious.

'The child is strong and active for one so young,' observes Aunt Gwyneth. 'It moves and kicks like a six-months baby.'

'It is clear that the Goddess has Her hand upon it,' agrees Aunt Olwen. 'Surely we need not doubt Evan? It is his child, after all.'

'We all desire the same goal,' Aunt Gwyneth pours Evan's coffee thoughtfully.

'But there might be many roads that lead to it,' points out Aunt Olwen.

There is a little silence. They feel uneasy but cannot tell why.

*　　　*　　　*

'What are you looking at?' asks Clarissa nervously. 'Why are you staring into the corner like that?'

Megan turns to look at Clarissa. Her small face is grave and she is troubled. She knows that she cannot tell her step-mother that the young chevalier who was stabbed in a duel on the terrace, and who is now standing by the chimney breast, only shows himself when a Mortimer is about to die. She knows that Clarissa will probably have hysterics if she should impart this fascinating piece of information to her, so she hesitates for a long moment, thus arousing Georgy's attention.

'Seeing one of your ghosts, are you?' she asks genially. 'Who is it this time?'

'Well yes,' says Megan, surprised at Georgy's intuition. 'Can you see him, too?'

'Please,' cries Clarissa desperately. '*Please.*'

'I thought you liked having all the old family about,' says Georgy flippantly. She is annoyed by a little scene she has witnessed enacted between Clarissa and Evan, very recently, and sees an opportunity to get her own back. 'You were saying the other day that you found them comforting.'

'That was the other day,' says Clarissa. She looks tired and drawn and her voice is edgy. 'I can't cope with it today. I feel that something awful is about to happen.'

This time it is Clarissa who surprises Megan. Clearly she has felt the atmosphere which the young chevalier emanates, although she cannot see him. Megan sighs to herself. Clarissa is a Mortimer by marriage and therefore might not be exempt. For herself, she is not worried. She knows that death is nothing but she is aware of unrest, of battles between the forces of darkness and light, of good and evil. Automatically her hand feels inside her shirt for the silver cross she wears on a long chain round her neck and her gaze returns to the pale shade in the corner by the chimney breast. Her lips move silently as she recites the words of the *De Profundis*: '*Out of the depths have I called unto Thee, O Lord . . .*'

'Come off it,' Georgy is saying to Clarissa, laughing incredulously. 'Gypsy Rose Lee tells your future if you cross her palm with silver. Where's your crystal ball, dearie?'

'Oh, shut up,' says Clarissa crossly. 'You're so insensitive sometimes. I think I have a kind of sixth sense . . .'

'Since when?' jeers Georgy. 'Pity you didn't have it in the old days, that's all I can say. All those losers and married men you picked up. It would have come in *very* useful.'

'Look who's talking,' says Clarissa resentfully, 'after your little *débâcle* in America. Anyway, I think it's something to do with being pregnant . . . Oh!'

She stops with a gasp, hand clapped to mouth, eyes on Megan. Even Georgy is jolted out of her bad temper. Megan, however, is oblivious to Clarissa's indiscretion and the two girls look at each other, mutual self-interest renewing the bonds of friendship.

'Twit!' mutters Georgy – but she grimaces with relief and starts to chuckle.

Clarissa laughs with her, glad that they are friends again, feeling a little less depressed.

'Come on,' says Georgy, knowing that she has been too outspoken as usual, 'finish up the shortbread.' She leans closer to her dear, best friend and mouths 'don't forget you're eating for two,' and they both collapse in silent giggles, their eyes on Megan's unsuspecting back.

All is well. Or is it?

Later, much later, Clarissa is standing by the door that leads to the gravelled court at the side of the house. Foreboding still presses closely upon her and she is not surprised to see that the sun has disappeared behind dark, menacing clouds. The thundery gloom accords with her mood. The birds are silent and a cold breeze springs up, stirring the bare branches of the trees. She notices that washing is still hanging on the line and she wonders that it has not been fetched in long since. She knows that she should take it down – the basket stands close by – before the rain comes, yet she is reluctant to leave the doorway. As she stands hesitating, she wonders where the aunts are. There is a deserted feel, not only outside in the grounds but behind her in the house, and the foreboding increases. Clarissa pulls herself together and steps out into the court; it is foolish to leave the washing to be soaked simply because she's having a silly fit of nerves.

As she drops the garments into the basket, she is surprised by the variety of clothing. These solid undergarments must belong to the aunts but whose are these flimsy silk chemises, wide-legged, with lacy trimming? Her sense of disquiet grows as these slip from her hands into the basket. They are Georgy's, of course, but . . . A sound behind her makes her jump. The door is swinging in the wind which is now rising and the leaves of the laurel bushes rustle, as though someone is moving behind them. Whose is that tall shadow by the wall? She quickly drags the remaining items from the line with trembling fingers, longing to be back inside, but as she turns she notices that there is a little chair, left by someone who has sat there in the sun earlier. Who would sit outside in November? Perhaps Evan sat there, smoking a cigarette in the morning sunshine?

She stares at the chair, unwilling to go further away from the house but knowing that she should not leave the cushion to get wet. She watches the movement of the laurel's branches, forcing back her fear, wishing one of the aunts would come out of the house. Swallowing nervously she hurries across to the chair and, in the moment that she bends to pick up the cushion, she knows that something has slipped behind her into the house. She knows that she should not have left the door unguarded and that, now, whatever was watching her has entered inside.

Clarissa clutches the cushion to her breast and tries to laugh. She is being quite ridiculous. It is all to do with her condition and with Megan's stories of ghosts. She will go back into the house and there will be nothing at all; it will be just as it always is. Inside the door she pauses, peering ahead into the gloom of the long passage. The wind catches the door out of her hand and slams it behind her and she wheels round with a gasp. Now there is darkness. She stands quite still, knowing with utter certainty that someone is in the passage with her. She sees the darker shadow against the gloom and she feels the terror rising in her throat. The shadow draws closer; a hooded figure, tall and menacing.

She tries to turn, to run away, back out into the grounds, but her legs are heavy and her feet drag weightily along the slate floor. She glances behind her, along the passage, and feels a great and terrifying force, sees two fierce eyes. She begins to scream but her throat is restricted by fear and no sound will come. The child struggles in her womb, as if it will leap out towards the figure who is now sweeping down upon her, and she closes her eyes, fainting with terror.

She can hear a terrible noise, a grunting, groaning cry, and then her hands are seized and she flings herself backwards, away from her assailant. Someone is bending over her, forcing her down, and when she opens her eyes she sees that it is Megan and realises that the harsh, grunting noise is issuing from her own mouth. The child leaps again, fighting and wrestling within her, as Megan leans over her, the silver cross falling free of her shirt as she shakes Clarissa into wakefulness.

'Wake up,' Megan is crying. 'Wake *up*, Clarissa. You are safe. It was a dream.'

Clarissa cries out with pain as the baby thrashes within her and she begins to weep as she feels the warmth of Megan's hands and sees the clear eyes looking into her own. She clasps the hands, gripping them, still weeping with relief.

'It was horrible,' she sobs. 'Oh, horrible. Someone was trying to kill me. And the baby wanted me to die. I felt it. Oh . . .'

She bursts out with violent crying again and Megan pulls her into her arms, holding her close, and, between them, the baby struggles, fighting desperately but weakly, until it finally subsides.

15

Clarissa does not immediately recover from her nightmare. She stays listlessly in bed, feeling weak and heavy. Megan returns to school but her heart is troubled. She remembers Clarissa's words about the baby, which until now she has simply discounted as part of the dream, but now she broods upon them. She thinks back to the moment when she knelt beside Clarissa, her arms about her, and recalls how solid she felt, how unwieldy and awkward to hug. At the time she had been too concerned for Clarissa to give it any thought, but now she ponders on those words, thinks about the shape of her step-mother's body. Is it possible that Clarissa is with child? If this is the case, Megan wonders why she has not been told about it. Surely nothing could be more wonderful? Yet even her father has said nothing. Perhaps he has not been told either? Maybe it has been decided that he is not yet fit enough to hear the news, although Megan feels that it must surely encourage him as nothing else could.

Although she considers all these things carefully, part of her cannot quite bring herself to believe in this baby; she cannot 'see' it in the future life of the house. She makes no serious attempt to do so. Sometimes she cannot help herself; the visions come, whether she will or no, just as the 'seeing' came whilst she was with Evan. Megan knows, however, that such power can be dangerous and she deliberately turns aside from it if she can. Yet occasionally it has proved helpful, such as on the afternoon when she 'saw' Clarissa in the grove. She decides to put the events of half-term out of her mind. If there is a baby then she will be told about it in due course. At the same time, she cannot forget the appearance of the chevalier. He was there just before her mother died and Megan wonders whose death he now foretells. She telephones to check that all is well at home and is told that everyone is fine – except that Clarissa is still feeling rather listless and tired – and Thomas is making good progress in London.

Megan realises that it could be a more distant Mortimer whose life is about to come to an end and finally she refers the whole thing to a Higher Authority and gives her mind to her work.

Georgy finds the nightmare scene rather difficult to handle and is impatient with the fuss Clarissa has made over it. After all, did *she* not have a similar experience at Hallowe'en? She seeks out Evan and repeats the whole dream as Clarissa has, unwisely, related it to her really, *really* best friend.

'Honestly,' says Georgy derisively. 'I mean crazy or what? I really loved the bit about my sexy knickers on the line with the aunts' thermals. Don't you think that a psychiatrist would have a field day?'

She sees that Evan is not responding quite as whole-heartedly as he might and she looks at him more closely. There is something withdrawn about him, as if he has closed himself to her internally whilst externally he continues to act out the part she would expect him to play. Her eyes narrow thoughtfully as she watches him working, varnishing some replaced woodwork. Could he possibly have decided to exclude her from his plans? She experiences anger and fear in equal parts.

'We must meet,' she says abruptly. 'I need to talk to you.'

'You can talk to me here,' he says, almost sullenly – and her fear increases.

'Not worried about Clarissa, are you?' she asks lightly. 'I promise you there's nothing wrong with her. It's just another excuse to skive in bed. Nightmares!' She snorts with disgust. 'She's simply looking for ways to make herself interesting.'

Evan pulls himself together, aware that Georgy has gauged his mood which is still unsettled after his encounter with Megan. He is anxious that she should suspect nothing and decides to distract her a little.

'She doesn't need to go to those lengths to make herself interesting,' he says provocatively. 'She's got quite enough going for her as it is.'

Georgy raises her eyebrows. 'Really?' she says. 'That's not what you were saying a few weeks ago. You said that you found fat, fair women boring.'

She pauses, remembering how he had gone on to compliment her on her thin, dark vitality.

Evan laughs softly to himself, knowing exactly what she is thinking.

'Women,' he says, 'will believe anything as long as it's flattering.'

Georgy has an overwhelming urge to pour varnish down the back of Evan's neck but she controls herself with an effort. 'So men like to imagine,' she says scornfully. 'When will they learn that women are far more manipulative? It's just that they're much more subtle about it.'

It is at this moment that Evan realises that he doesn't like Georgy very much. He accepts that she is amusing, stimulating and energetic but he knows suddenly that he will tire of her very quickly. This is irritating. It means that some of his plans will have to be rejected and he will have to do some more serious thinking, nevertheless he feels quite strongly that he must be resolute. He must also be cunning. He swallows down his irritation and dislike and makes himself smile.

'I wouldn't dream of arguing,' he says ruefully. 'Haven't I lived with a woman for more than twenty years? They sup up deviousness and cunning with their mother's milk. Men are beginners beside them.'

'It doesn't sound as if your wife was too clever,' retorts Georgy, unable to resist the dig even if it means contradicting herself. 'You seem to have led her a right old dance.'

'That may be so,' says Evan, standing up and stretching his back, 'but it is she who's abandoned me for her safe, steady lover while I'm left with no-one and, what's more, half my home and savings will be vanishing away into his bank account.'.

'Good grief!' Georgy is shocked out of her annoyance. 'Has she actually left you then?'

'She has indeed,' sighs Evan. In fact she left several weeks earlier but he has decided to play his cards close to his chest on this one. 'Gone away, she has, to his nice big house in north Wales and I'm the one who has to pay up on account of a few love affairs here and there.'

'That's a bit much, isn't it?' demands Georgy, on Evan's side again now just as he intended. 'If this man's been her lover all these years why should she get off scot free? You mustn't let her get away with it.'

'I have my boy and girl to think of,' says Evan reprovingly. 'It wouldn't be right to have Hywel and Angharad thinking badly of their mother. God knows it's difficult enough for them having a father who's . . .'

'An unfaithful, lying bastard,' supplies Georgy impatiently, when Evan seems rather at a loss for words. 'But why should she just walk off with her lover and half your worldly goods just so your Whatsit and Thingummy can be protected from the truth? They're not children, after all. It's iniquitous.'

'True,' says Evan, smiling to himself. 'But that's what I mean, you see, about women being devious. I thought I was deceiving her and all the time it was her deceiving me. And far more successfully.'

Georgy fumes silently for a few moments. If she and Evan have a future together she resents this unknown woman walking off with half of what would have been her, Georgy's, worldly goods. Knowing exactly what she is thinking, Evan purses his lips so as to prevent them from stretching into a grin. He wonders why, at this very moment when he has decided that the plan which involved Georgy is no longer viable, he should tell her that he is a free man. He gives a mental shrug. He has discovered that in this house of his ancestors events happen of their own volition and he is happy to go with the flow.

Unfortunately, Georgy is used to bending people and situations to her will and she has no intention of sitting back patiently. That kind of behaviour might suit spineless idiots like Clarissa but, as for herself, *she* intends to go on fighting. Now that she knows that Evan is free she becomes thoughtful. She runs over the plans he has already outlined to her and sighs impatiently. Everything depends on the baby. Until it is born and Thomas's reaction has been witnessed nothing can be finally decided.

'I hate waiting,' she cries involuntarily. 'I'm bored with all this inaction.'

'It'll get more exciting when Thomas comes home,' Evan says consolingly. 'It'll be the devil's own job keeping you and Clarissa out of his way until the baby's born. We're nowhere near out of the wood yet. I still don't quite see how we're going to pull this one off.'

'It's madness letting Thomas come home,' says Georgy crossly. She glances at him slyly. 'But perhaps it won't be for too long, eh? A little accident with his wheelchair, isn't that how you put it?'

He laughs with her but he is relieved when they hear the aunts talking in the passage and Georgy slips out of the farther door.

Clarissa, sitting by the fire in the drawing-room, cannot shake off the feeling of foreboding that has been with her ever since the day which culminated in the nightmare. She can remember it vividly and still finds that she is nervous of the shadowy passages and landings and finds it quite impossible to remain for any length of time alone in the small saloon. She hates the approach of evening and insists on having a night-light by her bed. In fact the only consolation is that the baby has been far less violent, less aggressive within her. In fact it is some days since she has been aware of its restless, exhausting presence. It has, no doubt, been subdued by the shock its mother has sustained.

Inert and depressed, Clarissa stares at the flames. She feels that the after-effects of the whole episode call for a visit to the doctor but she is afraid to go. The family doctor is one of Thomas's friends and, although he is rarely seen by the family in either his professional or private capacity, she knows that once she has been examined all hope of keeping anything secret from Thomas would be impossible. Even at the hospital she is well known. No doubt there are clinics where she could have a private consultation but, at the mere suggestion, the aunts are loud in their condemnation of such an idea. They can give her a tonic which will calm her and restore her energy. She must rest and be content. All will be well.

Clarissa pulls her shawl more closely about her shoulders and thinks about Megan. She is quite certain that she gabbled indiscreet words in her fear on that terrible night, yet Megan has said nothing. Perhaps she thought Clarissa was simply raving and that it was all part of the nightmare. She remembers how the baby leaped and kicked inside her as if it would rend her in its determination to escape from the womb. She'd had the feeling that it was some kind of duel between herself and the child and that only one of them would survive it. Clarissa thinks that perhaps she will die in childbirth and it is a premonition of this that makes her chill and heavy with foreboding.

Tears slide down her cheeks and she gives a violent start as someone leans over the back of the sofa and touches her shoulder. She screams throatily and Evan presses her arm more firmly, holding it in his strong, warm hand.

'I didn't mean to make you jump,' he says gently. 'My poor girl, weeping here alone. Whatever is it?'

His kind words simply have the effect of making the tears fall faster and Evan comes round the sofa and sits beside her, taking her hand, wiping away the tears with his handkerchief. She remembers how happy they were together for that sweet, short time and weeps harder. Oh why must her life be so complicated and frightening?

'Come then, come here,' he murmurs, safe in the knowledge that the aunts are keeping Georgy occupied in the kitchen. It has been their idea that he should look in on Clarissa before he goes home. He is, after all, the child's father and he has a way with women which, at the moment, might work in helping Clarissa to pull herself together. 'Poor darling,' he whispers as he slips his arm about her and holds her close. 'I'm here, you know, if you need me.'

'Oh, Evan,' blubs Clarissa, remembering now how very much she loved him before the wretched baby came, 'I'm so unhappy.'

'There now, there now,' he says, stroking back her tangled hair. 'You have no need to be. We shall get through all this and then you shall choose.'

'Choose?' She pauses in her weeping, puzzled by this word. 'Choose what?'

'You shall choose between Thomas and me,' he answers confidently. 'It shall be just as you want.'

There is a long silence and Evan stares about the room, hearing the echo of his words, wondering what on earth has made him say them. Clarissa is staring up at him, her mouth open in amazement.

'But,' she says childishly, 'but I thought you liked Georgy best.'

Evan laughs. He is surprised at how light-hearted he feels under the circumstances.

'Nonsense,' he says robustly. 'It was you who threw me over once you knew about the baby. You had no use for me then. You became cold and withdrawn. Just like my wife used to act to me once I had been useful to her. No wonder I turned to other women for love and kindness. And now she's gone off with her lover, leaving me alone.'

Evan stops talking and wonders if he has gone utterly mad. Never a one to commit himself, he has now as good as proposed to two women in one afternoon. The rake of the family, who was shot by a rival as he slept in his bed upstairs two hundred years previously, shakes his head as he lounges beside them, watching the scene with interest and amusement. Aunt Olwen, coming in to see how things are going, unobtrusively shoos him away and smiles at the two others sitting on the sofa close together.

'Now that's better,' she says approvingly. 'That's very nice.'

Clarissa goggles at her, surprised that Aunt Olwen isn't shocked to see her snuggling up to Evan. Then she remembers that the darling old aunts have always been deliciously broad-minded and giggles a little.

'I must be going,' says Evan as Aunt Olwen goes over to the drinks tray. He puts his mouth close to Clarissa's ear. 'That's a secret, mind. What I just told you. Just between you and me, yes?'

'Oh yes,' breathes Clarissa delightedly. 'Oh, *must* you go?'

'I'll see you tomorrow,' he promises aloud. 'Look after yourself.'

'We shall do that for her,' says Aunt Olwen, bustling over with a drink. 'No more miseries now?'

'No,' agrees Clarissa, simpering idiotically at Evan's departing figure. 'No more miseries.'

16

Tension increases as the days pass; each of the inhabitants watches and waits. Only the aunts have no secrets from each other. They want what is best for the house and the grove but they are still wondering who will stand as guardian between themselves and the child. They are beginning to think that Evan is the answer the Goddess has given them but cannot quite see how he might be properly used. He and Clarissa could make more children and the line would be protected; but what of Thomas? They need someone here in the house but how would it be possible to have Evan *in situ* with Thomas back at home? Clearly it is unthinkable. Nevertheless they have been trained to obedience and they wait, wondering when the way will be shown to them. Like Evan, they have more or less excluded Georgy from their plans. It seems that she has been sent merely as a way of bringing the baby into the family and after that she will have to go back to her own life.

They are relieved to see that Clarissa seems happier after Evan's attention and see no reason why they should not continue to be lovers after the baby has been born. Thomas will never be able to supply her physical needs so it seems perfectly reasonable to them that Evan should be his proxy. There must be no more babies, however. Both aunts know that Thomas will never countenance such obvious proof of his wife's unfaithfulness. No, Evan and Clarissa must be sensible, discreet, and all will be well. This does not answer the real problem, however. Who will bury them in the grove and continue to attend to the Goddess until the child is grown?

Georgy, untrained to exerting self-discipline, frets and fumes. She has the comfort of knowing that Evan is free but, like the aunts, she spends considerable time in brooding on how her own plans are to be achieved. At the beginning Evan outlined all sorts of schemes. It was always understood that Georgy would make herself indispensable to Clarissa – although she has been somewhat reckless on one or two occasions here – so that, whether Thomas is around or not, Georgy will be necessary. This, however, is the least favourite of all the plans. She prefers Evan's more ambitious ideas; the ones in which she and Evan finish up as master and mistress, with Thomas and Clarissa cleverly disposed of, although the baby would have to remain.

Getting rid of Thomas sounded a fairly simple operation when Evan talked of it at first and she even accepted that it was possible that Clarissa, with the help of the aunts' cordials and so on, might not last too long afterwards. Georgy is confident that with a strength of purpose anything can be accomplished. However, nothing must happen in a rush; suspicion must not be aroused. There are variations on the theme. One is that Clarissa should be got rid of and Georgy should work on Thomas's weaknesses so that she eventually becomes his wife. This leaves Evan in the background but with Thomas so restricted that might not be too much of a problem. Georgy can see how easy it might be to have Clarissa banished. She only has to tell Thomas the truth about the baby to have Clarissa sent packing but, in that scenario, it is reasonable to assume that the baby would go too and she knows that the aunts would have something to say to that.

A second variation is that Thomas should suffer some terrible accident which, in his damaged condition, would finish him off. Clarissa would lean heavily upon Georgy for companionship and advice and Evan could be brought in gradually until Clarissa was totally dependent upon them both . . .

Georgy sighs impatiently. She wants more than this and she wants it soon. Evan is evasive when she tries to pin him down, saying that he prefers to wait until the baby is born and Thomas home before any final decision is made. Georgy knows that this makes sense but she is beginning to find it difficult to keep pretending. It is even more difficult now that Clarissa seems to have revived a little and has an irritatingly smug and secretive air about her. She is still feeling tired and weak, however, and her inclination towards immobility gives Georgy the opportunity to bother Evan at his work with little fear of interruption. This morning when she bursts in on him there is someone with him; a girl who turns away quickly at her unexpected and precipitate arrival and fumbles in her bag. She seems distressed and Georgy stares at her curiously, guessing that this is Evan's daughter with the unpronounceable name.

Evan murmurs introductions but when Angharad turns Georgy sees that she has put on dark spectacles and she barely acknowledges Georgy's greeting before hurrying away, out of the French windows that lead onto the side terrace.

'Well,' says Georgy, surprised and intrigued. 'Why the Ray-Bans? What's her problem?'

'She's been crying,' says Evan. He sounds edgy, irritable. 'More trouble with her mother. Lover boy doesn't want Angharad in his cosy little nest and there's been a bit of a row. Angharad loves her mum but I'm afraid Hywel is the favourite and Angharad has always come a poor second. I've been telling her that I shall always have a home for her but the house is up for sale now and we'll have to look for something smaller together. She's taking it a bit hard, poor Angharad, losing her mum and her home all in a matter of weeks.'

Georgy is silent. There is no room for daughters in her schemes and she feels a resentment against Angharad. She doesn't blame Evan's wife and her boyfriend for not wanting the girl around in their new life together and she sees no reason why she should have her, either.

'I expect,' she says casually, 'that she'll be wanting a place of her own soon, won't she? Girls like to be independent, don't they? Has she got a boyfriend?'

Evan shakes his head, whistling between his teeth. 'Not like that, Angharad isn't,' he says comfortably.

'All girls are like that,' snaps Georgy. 'Don't be so daft.'

'She's very shy,' explains Evan. 'A real little home body. Cooks a treat, she does. I'll be glad to have her about.'

'And what about . . . later?' asks Georgy sullenly.

'Later?' Evan looks at her puzzled. 'Oh, *later*.' He laughs. 'We'll deal with that when it happens. No point crossing bridges.'

'Possibly not,' says Georgy, 'but I don't quite see how she'll fit into our plans. We didn't discuss her, if I remember rightly.'

'That's because none of this had blown up,' points out Evan reasonably. 'But she *is* my daughter, after all. She's my responsibility.'

'Pity your wife doesn't feel the same way,' mutters Georgy.

Evan gives her a long, level look. 'She's my child,' he says quietly. 'I love her.'

Georgy is silenced but her restlessness increases and she goes away to see if she can irritate and annoy Clarissa. Evan looks after her thoughtfully; another difficult corner has been successfully negotiated but he is still on edge.

Clarissa refuses to rise to Georgy's bait. She has all the comfort of knowing that she is the chosen one, that she cannot lose, that she has choices. Whilst she sits, idly watching the flames or fiddling at a piece of knitting, she thinks about the future. She knows that, when the time comes, she will find it almost impossible to exert herself to make such a momentous decision. Nevertheless it is very pleasant to dwell on all the possibilities. It is a tremendous relief to know that, should Thomas discover the truth, she will not find herself cast out alone in the world – yet the thought of leaving the house fills her with sadness. It is the house she fell in love with and married and she cannot bear the idea of losing it. On the other hand, there is Evan ... If only she could have the house *and* Evan, not to mention Evan's baby, her cup would be full and running over. She remembers what Georgy said about Thomas not surviving very long after such a severe accident and wonders if it is true.

She smiles at Georgy when she wanders in and curls up in an armchair opposite. Georgy stares at her, wondering if it is possible that Evan is two-timing her with Clarissa and, if he is, what to do about it. If Clarissa should decide to go off with Evan before the baby is born or Thomas is home there will be no role for her here. Her intuition tells her that Clarissa has some secret and she decides to put the boot in on the Evan front, just in case.

'How are you?' she asks, wriggling more comfortably between the wide arms of the chair. 'How's Ghengis?'

'I wish you wouldn't call the baby that,' says Clarissa, slightly put out. 'Anyway, the aunts insist that she's a girl.'

'OK,' says Georgy shrugging. 'It's only because you're always going on about what a bruiser it – she – is. Which do *you* want? Boy or girl?'

Clarissa hesitates. Part of her sees herself as the matriarch of some great dynasty; a mother of tall, handsome sons. Were not the Mortimers a powerful, ruling family: warriors and Marcher lords? Yet another part longs for a little girl that she can dress in sweet, pretty clothes and with whom she will be a great chum later on. They will go shopping together and this delightful daughter will tell her all her innermost secrets and bring home delicious young men with whom Clarissa will flirt. 'Oh, honestly,' they'll cry. 'You *can't* be Charlotte's? Sarah's? Sophie's? mother. I don't *believe* it. You look *far* too young. More like a sister . . .'

'Can't decide?' asks Georgy brightly, breaking into this delightful reverie.

'It would be rather fun to have a daughter,' admits Clarissa rather coyly. 'So much more of a friend than a son would be I should think. You can do jolly things with a girl, can't you? You can be really close.'

'Like you were with your Mum?' asks Georgy idly, knowing that Clarissa and her mother fought like cats.

Clarissa looks cross and Georgy grins privately as she hugs a cushion to her chest.

'I'd prefer a boy,' she says. 'Give me men every time. They'd bring home all their friends from school. Gorgeous hunks in the first fifteen. Anyway, they're so much less complicated than women. Look at poor old Evan all in a state about that wretched daughter of his.'

'Evan?' Clarissa sits up straight, knitting abandoned. 'What's this about his daughter? He hasn't said anything to me.'

Noting the sharp tone and repressing the urge to say 'Why should he?' Georgy raises her eyebrows.

'Oh, haven't you seen her?' she asks, surprised. 'She's always here whingeing on about something. Dreary little creature, if you ask me. You know that Evan's wife has left him? Yes? Well, apparently the new husband doesn't want darling little Annie-hang-yourself, or whatever she's called, messing up the works so she's got to live with Daddy. Good job Evan is such a devoted father, isn't it? Not that he seems quite so devoted about *your* child . . .'

Clarissa, however, is too concerned about Angharad to rise to the jibe.

'Oh, poor little girl,' she cries. 'How hurtful. Surely her mother has something to say about it?'

'Her mother doesn't want her either,' says Georgy indifferently. 'Personally, I can imagine just how she feels. *Too* embarrassing having a girl of twenty or so witnessing your love-making. Specially when she's the daughter of your cast-off husband, the girl's beloved father. Imagine the disapproval. Brrr!' Georgy shivers artistically and looks challengingly at Clarissa. 'Don't pretend *you* wouldn't mind.'

'But I didn't mind about Megan,' cries Clarissa. 'Why should I? Thomas *is* her father, after all. It would have been too cruel just after her mother died to have refused to have her in the house. I think it's disgraceful.'

Georgy is silent for a moment. She has completely forgotten about Megan.

'It was different for you,' she says, rallying. 'To begin with, Megan is away at school most of the time and secondly, this was her home long before it was yours. Not quite the same, is it?'

'I suppose not,' says Clarissa slowly. 'But I can still feel sorry for her. I think Evan told me that the brother is the favourite. Of course, he's older. He doesn't live at home any more. Poor – what did you call her?'

Georgy shrugs. 'Can't pronounce it,' she says. 'Some outlandish Welsh name. Haven't you ever seen her?'

'No,' says Clarissa, almost indignantly, hurt that Evan has been keeping his daughter from her. 'I shall ask Evan to introduce us next time she comes.'

'Oh, he won't do that,' says Georgy. 'She's one of these shrinking violets. Won't look you in the eye and leaps out of the door or into the car if she hears you coming. Comes rushing out to Daddy every time anything upsets her. Pathetic, really.'

'That's what comes of being unloved,' says Clarissa sententiously. 'Poor child . . .'

'Oh, Evan loves her,' Georgy assures her. 'He told me that she comes first in his life. Love me, love my daughter. Whoever Evan marries will have to cope with his dear little Welsh cake, too.'

Clarissa is thoughtful, staring at the fire. She is attempting to fit this girl into her dreams of life with Evan. 'She's not still at school then?' she asks.

'Don't know,' says Georgy. 'She can drive. She's got a little car. I expect darling Daddy bought it for her.'

Clarissa smiles at her really, *really* best friend. 'I don't think you need to get upset about it,' she says gently. 'I have a feeling that this girl will never be a problem for you.'

There is a smugness, a faint emphasis on the word 'you' which sets Georgy's teeth on edge and for a moment she can think of nothing to say.

'A daughter,' says Clarissa confidently, settling comfortably to her knitting again. It's easier to be fond of the baby now it seems to be less violent. 'I've made up my mind that I'd really love a little girl.'

17

All too soon the work is finished on Thomas's new quarters and there is no longer any excuse for Evan to come to the house. For obvious reasons it is difficult, with both girls there, for him to come merely as a friend or even as a relative. This has never been the way of the relationship and so it seems that Evan must go back to his more distant role. In different ways each of the four women miss him. Since the excuse for visiting Thomas cannot be used, Georgy tries to think up good reasons for going to the town and puts pressure on the aunts to have the car insured for her to drive. She points out that it would be sensible in case of emergencies and so that she could take Clarissa for little rides, but obstacles are put in her way – '*much too cold to go out driving*' – or procrastination – 'we really must look into it. Perhaps tomorrow . . .' – and nothing gets done.

Clarissa has had several private moments of an intimate and loving nature with Evan before his work is done and she is able to relax peacefully, content to wait. She misses him but knows that although Georgy misses him, too, she is unable to visit him, thanks to the aunts' stance regarding the car. Evan has implied that Georgy has become a bit of a nuisance, pestering him and so on, and Clarissa is once again overwhelmed with love for him, delighted that he is unmoved by Georgy's attractions. Poor old Georgy just doesn't seem to be able to make it with the chaps; just hasn't got what it takes. Clarissa sighs with sheer pleasure, still pondering on how she can possibly achieve Evan, the baby and the house, all in one package. There would be plenty of room for Megan and Angharad – Clarissa thinks it's *such* a pretty name – to muck in together, especially as Megan will be off to the convent for good in a year or so. Guessing that Evan has been made aware of Georgy's opinions she has taken care to assure him that, if *they* ever have a home together, there will always be room for Angharad who, she discovers, is training to be a nurse. At present she lives in but she likes to come home when she is off-duty and when her training is finished she will need a roof over her head. Evan is clearly moved by Clarissa's unselfish attitude and kisses her gratefully. Clarissa is big with generosity and radiates love – especially towards poor old Georgy.

The aunts miss Evan, too. It has been fun to have a kinsman about the place who understands their little ways and is ready to help them to achieve their goals. They decide that there is much of dear Mama in Evan and hope he has passed on these genes to Clarissa's child. They still have no idea as yet as to where the Goddess is leading them but they plan to make great efforts for Her during the celebration of the winter solstice. It amuses them to see how readily Christianity has appropriated the old pagan festival but it suits their purpose, although they wonder if Clarissa really has any idea that the ancient fire-festival of midwinter survives in the yule log which she insists must be fetched from the woods ready for Christmas.

Even Georgy is mollified by the preparations for Christmas, especially when Evan is called upon to deal with yule logs and Christmas trees and other heavy tasks, and a few trips to the town help to dispel boredom even though the aunts are present.

It is during the quiet days, whilst the house is occupied with cooking and cleaning and making ready for Thomas's arrival, that the aunts become aware of the newcomer. No ghost this but real, powerful flesh and blood whose proximity fills them with exhilaration and hope. They have felt her presence once or twice already during the past months but until now it has been a fugitive sensation: a soft footfall; a sharp intake of breath; the flick of a skirt disappearing round a corner. Now they see her shadow at the end of the drive, in the grounds, within the walls of the house itself and their hearts beat fast with anticipation; at last the waiting seems to be coming to an end. It comes much more dramatically than any of them could begin to imagine.

When Thomas arrives home it is as if a convulsion in time has taken place. The aunts insist on fetching him, rather than having hospital transport, and in the end the whole business is rather peremptory. The best having been done for Thomas, he is passed over to the care of his family with very little ceremony. Only the matron continues to be helpful and supportive and gives minute instructions for his comfort and welfare. Thomas has progressed as well as everyone has hoped but no more time and money can be spent on him and he must go home. The aunts explain that poor Clarissa is not well, that she is run down, and imply that it is an after-effect of dedicated visiting and so much anxiety about her husband. This is readily accepted by both Matron and Thomas but everyone is feeling nervous by the time Thomas is helped from the car into his wheelchair and they push him into the house.

The moment that Clarissa sees him she realises that all her hopes and dreams are so many castles in the air. She has been living in a bubble, out of time, and she knows that it will be impossible to attempt to deceive him. She perceives how much of a force he is, even in a wheelchair. Pain and frustration have done their work on him. He is much thinner, yet energy seems to emanate from him; his jaw is sharp, his mouth clamped with determination into a narrow line like split slate, his eyes . . . It is in his eyes that Clarissa sees the greatest change. The grey seems to flicker and shine, like bright light striking cold sea water; their fierce stare seems to penetrate her skull, seeking out her secrets, detecting her lies, probing her weaknesses. After the first awkward embrace, once she stands back to look at him, she is terrified. How did they imagine that they could deceive him for a single moment?

Sensing her panic, the aunts attempt to protect her. They, too, see that Thomas has changed or, rather, that this tragedy has strengthened other sides of his character and they are glad that it has been agreed that Georgy shall remain out of sight for the time being until Thomas has settled in. As she looks at Thomas, Clarissa remembers how the four women laughed together as they practised padding Georgy out so as to look pregnant. Already it is as if it were in another lifetime, years past. She swallows nervously as she answers Thomas's questions – quite innocuous questions, it is her guilt which lends them a sinister light – and shows him his new quarters. All these months it has seemed as if the house were her own, that she had the right to plan and arrange its future, now she sees how futile her hopes have been. Crippled though he is, Thomas comes back into his home like a king entering into his inheritance. It is where he belongs.

'You've put on weight,' he says, studying her. 'You haven't been pining for me, that's clear.'

'Oh, honestly,' she cries, flushing with embarrassment and terror. 'Of course I've missed you. It's just . . . I've been a bit unwell . . .'

She glances desperately at the aunts who rise to the occasion.

'She's been worn out with worrying about you,' says Aunt Olwen cheerfully, 'so we've been making her rest.'

'Too much shortbread,' says Thomas, who is determined to be cheerful and is delighted to be home again, although the thought of being restricted to two rooms – even such big rooms – fills him with a terrible depression. 'Well, we'll soon change all that. You wait until you've pushed me all over the grounds. You'll be as thin as a rake.'

They all laugh – rather too quickly and too heartily – at his simple little joke but Clarissa is not deceived. She knows that she has forgotten the flesh and blood Thomas, her real husband, the owner of the house, and all her future plans have been made around a cardboard cut-out, a doll which she imagined could be manipulated as she and her fellow conspirators wished. How readily she listened to them when they told her that all would be well; how easy it was to be deceived. Now she stands alone, helpless and afraid.

Thomas has learned to be as self-sufficient as possible and he can do a great deal for himself. Clarissa feels nervous and shy with him although she knows the extent of his injuries from the hours she has spent at the hospital. When he hears that she intends to sleep upstairs he is clearly disappointed. She does not know what might be in his mind, after all he has never been particularly physically inclined and now that he can't . . . She balks at imagining what he wants from her and once again the aunts save her.

'A bit of an infection,' murmurs Aunt Gwyneth. 'She wouldn't want to pass it on to you. It will soon clear up. She has to have plenty of sleep.'

She implies that Clarissa's sleeping arrangements are temporary and Thomas, though obviously put out, does not dispute it. He is too happy to be back at home to spoil this first night but it is evident that he intends to be master in his own house.

The aunts watch him closely. Even they are feeling less confident that they can bring off this enormous deception. The introspective hopelessness he displayed in hospital is gone. His time at the clinic has given him new hope and he intends to put up a fight. The aunts begin to wonder how they will achieve their plans, knowing that Clarissa is a weak link, aware of Georgy's ambitions. They do not show their anxiety, however, and Thomas is unaware of any undercurrents.

Clarissa retires early, leaving Thomas to the care of his aunts, and goes to see Georgy who has had supper alone on a tray and has gone up to bed. Forgetting all their differences and petty jealousies, Clarissa bursts out in a fit of weeping. She tells the surprised and fascinated Georgy of the changes in Thomas and of her fears for the future. Georgy is quiet, taking it all in, rapidly adjusting her ideas. She attempts to calm Clarissa, unwilling to say too much until she has had a chance to test the water for herself. This new dominant, fierce Thomas interests her. He doesn't sound a bit like the dull, middle-aged pussycat who has been described to her previously and she wants to be alone to brood on this new development. She sympathises warmly, tries to console Clarissa and finally shoos her off to bed.

Alone in her bedroom, frightened and feeling ill, Clarissa remembers her nightmare. She is reminded of that terrible weight of helpless terror, the panic of being pursued. Perhaps Thomas was the shadow who waited for her, who watched and threatened her. The thought of his discovering the truth makes her tremble and she begins to cry again. All is hopeless. She has forgotten that she can fly to Evan. With his departure, his influence has waned and now that Thomas has returned she feels helpless, powerless, unable to think or act independently. All she can do is weep. At last she falls asleep, exhausted, and once more begins to dream. This time the images are less clear if just as frightening. She is lost, running down endless passages, pursued by nameless horrors. When she wakes, her back aches and she has strange pains in her gut. Tossing and turning, sweating with fear, she remembers how the baby tried to leap from her womb during that other nightmare, how it seemed ready to rend and kill her, and now, quite suddenly, she recalls her premonition. Another terror seizes her, along with a stronger stab of pain and she begins to shout.

It is Georgy who comes to her this time and, when she sees what is happening, she runs for the aunts. It seems that nothing can help Clarissa. She has gone into premature labour but the baby will not be born. The aunts cannot quieten her, their potions cannot ease her and, when they beg her to be silent, she remembers how they have told her that she cannot have medical help lest her secret is discovered, and then she begins to scream in earnest. She is convinced that she will die and she no longer cares who knows about the baby. Even Thomas is roused by her screams and in the end, at his insistence, the doctor is called out.

When dawn breaks silence falls upon the house. Clarissa, heavily sedated, sleeps in her big bed. The baby has at last been expelled from her womb and has been wrapped in some linen and taken away. It has been dead, apparently, for some weeks, although it is not clear why. The doctor – Thomas's old chum – is confused by the two elderly women who manage to convince him that none of them realised that Clarissa was pregnant. He is too tired and shocked, too concerned with what he is about to tell Thomas, to take it all in properly. After all, the Mortimers have always been a strange, reclusive brood. It doesn't occur to him to think about the age or size of the baby relevant to Thomas's accident. He simply assumes that the child is Thomas's; poor Thomas, who has yet another wife prone to miscarriages, and who is in no fit state to hear such sad news. The doctor gently explains that the child has been dead in the womb for a while but for how long he isn't too sure. At least, he says comfortingly, Clarissa will recover. He knows that he cannot offer the consolation of more children.

There is no reason for Thomas to believe that it is not his child; it is simply another baby who has not survived. It is not a happy homecoming but at least Thomas is distracted from his own frustrations by these unexpected developments and by his concern for Clarissa's recovery. Georgy is now able to be introduced as Clarissa's friend who has been invited for Christmas and Evan – hearing the news by telephone – begins to consolidate his other, private plans.

On the eve of the winter solstice a tiny coffin, carefully packed with stones, is buried in the small churchyard on the hill. Much later, the body of the baby is buried with its ancestors in the grove. It is a freezing, moonless night; the standing stones are ghostly white. Black twigs are rimed with glittering frost and the ground creaks and cracks as the hooded figures bend and bow before the granite slab on which a small box waits to be committed to the cold dark earth. The lamps flicker, sending strange shadows dancing out before their yellow light.

To the onlooker, hidden in the trees, it is as if the child's spirit is already abroad in the grove, being welcomed by its ancestors as an added force, another brooding presence, a new, vital power. From somewhere distant, outside the grove, she senses another very different power, an opposing force of light and purity which has already nearly defeated them, and she calls on all her strength, closing out this unwelcome presence, summoning help against it. The icy air rings with unearthly voices, the spirits crowd closer and a yet deathlier chill, rising like mist, curls around the standing stones and enters the grove.

She bows her head, covering her face before the coming of the Goddess, and, when she next dares to look, the box is gone.

18

For several weeks Clarissa is ill; a kind of minor breakdown after the terror and pain. It is fortunate that she remains in bed, curtains drawn, refusing company and food, for she feels no remorse for the dead baby and she cannot pretend to mourn it. Even now, she feels there was a battle between herself and the child, a battle from which only one of them would emerge. Occasionally, she remembers, she was able to convince herself that she would bear a normal baby but she tells herself that this was a delusion and she is relieved to be free of the incubus which inhabited her womb. She is too ill to follow the procession behind the coffin but later that night wakes from another terrible nightmare in which she dreams that she is being imprisoned in the earth beneath the standing stones. She tastes the grit and the mud and feels the weight crushing her bones. Her groans and struggles disturb Megan who comes to her, as she did before, and holds her in her arms.

As she feels peace flow over her, Clarissa has some dim idea that it is Megan – or rather Megan's faith – which killed the baby. She remembers how, on that awful night, the silver cross pressed sharply into her abdomen and how the baby slowly became subdued and, from that moment, never moved again. As she sees Megan's calm eyes looking into hers she feels a deep gratitude that it is all over.

'I was possessed by a devil,' she says sleepily.

'Hush,' says Megan gently.

'It raged about inside me,' continues Clarissa, rousing herself a little, knowing a sudden urge to communicate, 'seeking whom it may devour,' she adds, becoming biblical.

Megan is silent, thinking of the grove and the standing stones, knowing that there is quite enough evil ready at hand without calling it up and giving it fancy names. She feels the blood of her ancestors beating in her veins and knows now why the chevalier appeared, although she still does not realise that the baby was Evan's.

'You are safe,' she says calmly, feeling the Little One hovering close beside her, hoping that someone will be able to watch over the house once she has gone into the convent. As she waits for Clarissa to subside into sleep she keeps her gaze on the flickering night-light and, presently, Megan sees a vision of the grove. In the small white flame she watches the hooded figures moving about the altar and slowly she becomes aware of a third figure who is deliberately attempting to block her Sight. The two opposing forces lock, as they did on the night of Clarissa's nightmare, but this time it is Megan who gives way before the combined powers arrayed against her. She concentrates hard as the scene begins to fade until she finds that she is merely staring at the tiny flickering flame of Clarissa's night-light.

Her inexperience and innocence are no match for such force. Confused and anxious, Megan lowers the sleeping Clarissa gently onto her pillows and bends her own head in silent prayer.

The aunts are glad to have the excuse of Clarissa's illness to allow the time to pass without questions or recriminations. They know that Clarissa would crumble very quickly under any pressure and they continue to be vague with Thomas until the danger is past. As for themselves, they are puzzled as to why the child died. The ways of the Goddess are strange indeed and now they try to find answers for the events of the last year.

'Then why is Georgy here?' ponders Aunt Olwen. 'She is no longer required, it seems now that she never was. So why was she sent?'

'It might have been coincidence,' suggests Aunt Gwyneth. 'We may have misunderstood Her plans. Though why the child should die . . . ?'

They are silent, brooding. Nothing seems to make sense; Thomas crippled; Clarissa childless. From where will the next guardian come? Simultaneously, they become aware of the vital new presence, somewhere near at hand, and their eyes meet, questioning, careful. They move quietly about the house, alert, waiting, dealing with Thomas's needs, ministering to Clarissa, getting Megan back to school. It is as if they work with an ear cocked, eyes darting, eager for confirmation of the new atmosphere that seeps into the house.

Clarissa recovers slowly but she is depressed, unwilling to be comforted or cheered. There is no word from Evan and, sunk as she is in despondency, she makes no effort to contact him. On her few excursions downstairs, Thomas finds that it is *he* who is obliged to make the effort to raise *her* spirits which is faintly irritating under the circumstances. Georgy hastens to show solidarity with him. She spends a great deal of time with him whilst the aunts are busy and he finds her company stimulating and soothing. She understands just how he feels and shows it in an off-hand, understated manner which suits his mood. Although his accident has hardened him, he is slightly put out to find his position of invalid superseded by Clarissa's.

'Rather bad luck for you to come home to all this,' Georgy says sympathetically as they lunch together.

Clarissa is having lunch in bed and the aunts have gone

to the town, shopping. Georgy makes no attempt to go with them to find Evan; she has other fish to fry.

'Oh, I'm OK,' says Thomas shortly. When he is with Georgy, his old characteristics tend to make a bit of a come-back and he feels just a little sorry for himself. He will not be disloyal to his wife, however. 'Poor Clarissa. What a rotten thing to have happened. Especially now that . . .'

He hesitates. They are not on familiar enough terms to discuss his inability just yet but Georgy lowers her eyes tactfully and murmurs politely, indicating that she is aware of the problems.

'She's always been rather highly strung,' she says thoughtfully. 'All these nightmares and so on. Megan rather frightened her with the stories of ghosts.' She laughs lightly, the laugh of one who does not believe in such nonsense. 'So silly.'

'A house as old as this one and with its history is bound to have a few reverberations,' says Thomas fairly, 'and some people are more sensitive than others . . .'

'Oh quite,' says Georgy quickly. She does not wish to sound uncharitable. 'That's absolutely true. But there's a dignity here. A terrific history. It's not quite the spooks-in-white-sheets stuff, is it? We're talking about a fantastic heritage. I really envy you.'

Thomas looks at her, impressed with her sensible accept-ance and good taste.

'There are so many legends handed down,' he says, putting his knife and fork together on his plate. 'So many stories that Megan has heard from babyhood upwards. No doubt she thought that Clarissa would be interested.'

'Oh, it isn't *Megan's* fault,' says Georgy – and pauses, wondering how far she can go. 'Megan has a true sense of the past. *She* doesn't have nightmares.'

'Of course, this is her home,' says Thomas, smiling his thanks as Georgy removes his plate and pushes the pudding trolley within his reach. She is clever enough never to fuss over him or to deny his independence. 'She's used to it. So are my aunts. It must be hard for someone coming to it new. Even I have my superstitions.'

'Don't we all,' agrees Georgy. 'Let me help you to some cream.'

'I understand you've known Clarissa since school days,' says Thomas, digging into his apple pie.

'Oh, forever,' agrees Georgy. 'She's been so sweet since my . . . well, *you* know.'

'Well,' hesitates Thomas. 'I *don't* quite know . . . not that I want to pry . . .'

'I realise that,' says Georgy with a grateful look – she has not quite yet decided what story she might tell him and she doesn't want Clarissa putting her foot in it later. 'How kind you are. And I'm so grateful that you're allowing me to stay here in this wonderful house. It has such a healing atmosphere. I was wondering whether we might go for a stroll after lunch? It's quite mild and you could show me round. Clarissa's not much of a one for the great outdoors so I've hardly been outside.'

'I should love it,' says Thomas, who misses his outdoor life terribly. 'If you don't mind coping with the chair?'

'Don't be silly,' laughs Georgy. 'It'll be fun. Shall I make the coffee?'

Clarissa watches them from her bedroom window. She has decided that she feels well enough to go downstairs and has been visited with the noble and uplifting thought that she will sit with Thomas. The poor darling must be so bored and she feels confident now that the subject of the baby will not be broached. The aunts have told her that, due to the confusion, Thomas believes that the child was his and, apart from his natural disappointment, the whole thing may be safely ignored. If they are surprised at Clarissa's quiet acceptance they make no mention of it and, after poor Claerwen, Thomas is used to such blows. Life, it seems, must take up where it left off, although it can never be quite the same again.

Clarissa is rather shocked when she realises that nearly a month has passed. She knows that she has been ill but now she is beginning to feel stronger and to wonder what she will do with herself. Pushing aside her tray and rising from the bed, she decides that she must devote her time to Thomas. She finds it almost impossible to think about Evan. Whilst she is here, in this house, he seems so far away, so unreal. Anyway, he has made no attempt to communicate with her; not even a scribbled line or some flowers after she lost the baby. Weak tears of self-pity fill her eyes. It was, after all, his child . . .

Pulling herself together, she realises that it might be very awkward for Evan to contact her now that Thomas is back. The aunts *could* have acted as go-betweens but she suspects that, at the sight of the real, flesh and blood Thomas, their dreams collapsed just as her own did. They were all living in a fantasy world. She dresses slowly, wandering between wardrobe and chest, and it is thus, as she pauses to glance out of the window, that she sees Thomas in his chair being wheeled across the lawn by Georgy. Their progress is slow and it is obvious that the grass is wet and the going is heavy. Georgy bends to her task, laughing and Clarissa sees Thomas's bright cheerful face, his head flung back so that the two of them seem almost to be kissing . . .

For one silly, childish moment she is tempted to hammer crossly on the window; to shout 'What *do* you think you're doing? That's *quite* enough of that . . .' but commonsense restrains her and she moves back, watching as they disappear from view, her thoughts jumbled and confused. It is perfectly reasonable to assume that Thomas and Georgy must have been thrown together a great deal during the last few weeks. Naturally they have become friendly; why not?

Moving back into the bedroom, Clarissa can think of a good number of reasons why not. She knows now that she does not truly love Thomas but he is *her* husband, not Georgy's. It is not that she wants to go out in a cold winter afternoon playing nursemaid but she doesn't care to see quite such a jolly camaraderie developing between Thomas and her really, *really* best friend. The scene had such a cosy domestic air about it; really, one would think that Georgy lived here, had just as many rights and privileges as she, Clarissa, the rightful wife and chatelaine. It is time that Georgy was planning her own future: time she moved on. She pulls on a cardigan sulkily and wishes that the aunts were there to comfort and cheer her although, now that she thinks of it, they are not *quite* as solicitous as they were when she was still with child. They have nursed her wonderfully, no question – kindly, patient, thoughtful for her wellbeing – but that special attention, as if she were a clever, dearly loved child, has been absent of late.

Clarissa fastens her shoes thoughtfully. Perhaps it is simply that with Thomas home there isn't quite so much time to spare. The poor old dears must be rushed off their feet. She thinks with longing of those jolly times in the small saloon; coffee and shortbread, tea with little tasty treats, delicious drinks before dinner. Standing up straight, smoothing back her hair, she attempts to pull herself together. No doubt, once she is back in circulation, things will go on as before . . . Even as she tries to convince herself, she hears the car chugging up the drive and her heart soars upward. The aunts are home in time for tea and she goes hurrying down to meet them.

Tea *is* a very jolly affair, though not in the way that Clarissa is remembering. To begin with she is surprised to see that Thomas is not confined to his two large rooms. He has taken a careful survey of the house and has seen at once how other alterations can be made. He cannot think why they hadn't been thought of before and the aunts have to bluff their way through various reasons which he discounts as nonsense. When Clarissa comments on these changes, pretending to be delighted, he shakes his head in disgust.

'That builder of yours wants his head examined,' he says. 'I'd like a word with him but Aunt Gwyneth says he's moved on.'

'So he has,' agrees Aunt Olwen calmly, pouring tea. She shoots a warning glance at Clarissa who stares at her, eyes wide and questioning. Imperceptibly Aunt Olwen nods her head, lips pursed. 'Gone away to Malvern,' she says with a nice blend of irritation and resignation. 'Apparently his daughter has a job nursing over that way and they've gone together. Mother went off with another man or something. Quite a sad story, really.'

'Well, he hasn't much imagination,' says Thomas, accepting his tea. 'His work is first class, I'll say that, but there's much more he could have done.'

'He blinded us with science, didn't he, girls?' says Aunt Olwen cheerfully. 'All those rules and regulations about listed doorways and goodness knows what. He had good recommendations, though.'

'Oh, he's done well enough,' says Thomas handsomely, 'but I'm not stuffing in two rooms.'

'Certainly not, dear boy,' beams Aunt Olwen.

Clarissa takes her cup drearily, wondering if the dear old ancestors are clustering about. They must be thrilled to have the head of the house back amongst them. She finds herself wishing that Megan could be there with her. Despite her odd ways, there's something about Megan that makes her feel safe. As she sips her tea she realises that the focus of the attention is no longer on herself; it is on Thomas. Sitting on the sofa, his wheelchair tucked out of sight, with Georgy beside him and the aunts in attendance, he is like a king surrounded by courtiers. She experiences a poignant sense of loss – and fear. Georgy smiles across at her but there is something akin to triumph in her face and Clarissa's heart sinks further. She feels abandoned.

The aunts watch her, eyes bright and knowing. They have had a communication which has given them a whole new perspective on their problem. Slowly, they must go slowly, but they are excited and eager to pave the way ahead carefully and thoroughly. Georgy leans to replenish Thomas's cup and he smiles at her almost intimately. Clarissa bites her lip angrily, tears not far away, and the aunts exchange a bright, brief glance. There is much work to be done.

19

Winning Thomas's heart is much more difficult than Georgy imagines. He might have been caught off guard once, after Claerwen's death, bewitched by Clarissa's seductive light-heartedness, but he is not to be so deceived again. It is very pleasant to have an attractive young woman dancing attendance – and sheer good manners require that he makes a chivalrous response – but he is not taken in a second time. Thomas's brush with death has strengthened his need of his home and his own people. He is more sensitive to the atmos-phere of the house and remembers the legends concerning the oak groves and woods and how they have always been linked with the fortunes of his family. Confined, with so much time at his disposal, he often has strange thoughts and undefined longings.

He is sad that Megan will be entering the convent in the summer but he has promised and she is unswerving in her vocation. He knows that Claerwen would have wanted it and feels even more inclined than formerly to honour the traditions of her family. Yet he longs for his own people. He feels closer than he has ever been to the aunts but he realises that they cannot live for ever. To his dismay, Clarissa seems like a stranger to him and he cannot understand why he is not more upset about the baby. Surely a baby would have drawn them closer together? He would have been able to watch his child growing up, a consolation for Megan's loss, an heir for the house and the estate. To whom will it pass when he dies?

As for Georgy, he enjoys her company, she makes him laugh, but it is nothing more than that. He senses that Clarissa is resentful of the friendship that has grown up between them but he is not inclined to take her sulks seriously. Now that she is better she will see for herself that he has been merely playing the part of a good host to a special guest. After all, she *is* his wife's best friend. Nor does he suspect Georgy of attempting to cause trouble. He may be tougher, more introspective, but he is still fairly simple where women are concerned.

Georgy, however, has no intention of giving up. It might be more of a struggle than she hoped but she is convinced that she is making headway. She has shelved all thoughts of Evan for the present. It is clear that his daughter means more to him than either she or Clarissa and he is, therefore, not worth worrying about, especially now that Thomas is here before her. Although there are obvious disadvantages in being married to a cripple, they are outweighed by other considerations. The house is still the greatest attraction. Georgy has been taken in by Thomas's response to her. She is convinced that, if Clarissa were out of the way, he would turn to her for companionship. It does not bother her that she will never have children, she is not in the least maternal, but she craves the status her position as Thomas's wife would bring. As Clarissa did before her, she imagines filling the house with her friends, showing it off to its advantage, basking in admiration and envy. What an idiot her dear best friend has been to risk it all for a fling with Evan. Convinced that Thomas is becoming attached to her, she decides to do a little work on Clarissa.

'So how are you feeling?' she asks solicitously, joining her in the drawing-room in the hours between tea and dinner. 'Cold, isn't it?'

She pokes up the fire and adds a log or two. Once again Clarissa feels the irritation of one whose position is being usurped and she steels herself to speak openly.

'I expect you've been making some plans while I've been ill,' she begins brightly. 'It was good of you to hang on but I bet you're dying to get on with your life. Will you go back to America?'

It is now that Georgy realises that she has been a fool. She has been over-confident and reckless and might very well have spoiled everything. She should have been more careful of Clarissa's feelings instead of venting her frustration by winding up her best friend at every opportunity. She should have played Clarissa along until she was absolutely sure of Thomas and then dealt her the death blow. As it is, she is not nearly secure enough to risk a confrontation. She thinks quickly.

'I might,' she says casually. 'I haven't quite decided yet. Naturally I wanted to see you up and about again before I disappeared. Obviously all our plans have changed but I didn't know whether you needed me or not. I wouldn't want to leave you in the lurch.'

Clarissa is slightly wrong-footed by this approach. Georgy seems indifferent as to whether she stays or goes, not at all as if she has designs on Thomas. Then, too, she has made Clarissa feel ungrateful. After all, she was prepared to enter into the deception about the baby just so as to get her best friend out of a jam. She has been, thinks Clarissa guiltily, a brick.

'I can see,' Georgy is saying, 'that it's rather different now Thomas is back and you're better. I expect you want me out of your hair. Perfectly understandable but you'll have to give me time to get organised. I've rather cut myself off while I've been here and I had no idea how long I might be wanted . . .'

'For heaven's sake,' cries Clarissa, feeling an utter worm,

'there's no rush at all. Honestly. It's just I thought you were probably fed up with nothing to do except push Thomas about in his chair.'

'Oh well, I feel a bit sorry for the poor old boy,' she makes Thomas sound about a hundred, 'and it was the least I could do. Try to jolly him along a bit. Of course, I don't know what he looked like before his accident but I was expecting a younger looking man. He looks much older than his age, doesn't he? Did he always?'

Clarissa hesitates, taken aback and trying to remember what Thomas looked like before. *Does* he look much older? She feels faintly defensive.

'I don't quite know,' she says – and even she can hear how foolish it sounds. 'I never really noticed.'

Georgy arches her eyebrows. 'How sweet,' she says. 'Must be love. He's really nice, don't get me wrong, but he looks more like your father than your husband. All those lines on his face. Of course that might be due to the pain and stuff. And his hair has got lots of grey in it. How old is he?'

'Nearly forty-three,' says Clarissa stiffly. 'Actually he's younger than Evan.'

'You don't say,' marvels Georgy. 'He looks much older, doesn't he? Of course fair people wear better. Look at you, lucky old thing, you look far younger than me.'

'Nonsense,' mutters Clarissa, now thoroughly confused but flattered. 'Of course I don't . . .'

'Oh, I can bear it,' says Georgy cheerfully. 'I'm used to being the plain one. But I must say I can see why you had your little moment of passion with Evan. He's rather gorgeous, isn't he? What a pity he's moved away. All because of that dreary daughter with the weird name. Shame. You could have had a bit of fun now and again.'

'Honestly,' says Clarissa, forgetting that she'd had the same idea herself. 'As if I would . . .'

'Why ever not?' demands Georgy. 'You'll have to have

some fun. You can't bury yourself here for the rest of your life with a cripple and two old maids.'

'Sssh!' whispers Clarissa, glancing towards the door and giggling nervously. 'Honestly, Georgy. You are awful sometimes.'

'No I'm not,' says Georgy indignantly. 'I just care about you, that's all. We've had some fun, haven't we? A few laughs. But what will you do when I've gone?'

Clarissa tries to remember what it was like before Georgy turned up. Of course, she was receiving special treatment then, the new bride and then being pregnant, but how will it be now? The evenings will be long and dull again, no friends dropping in, no chance of having a baby . . . Depression begins to steal over her and tears threaten.

Watching her, Georgy sees that she'll never have the energy to make decisions or control her own life. Impatience rises but she wills it down. It seems that Clarissa will never leave of her own free will, why should she? Boredom is preferable to many other fates – working, for instance – and Clarissa has always been idle. Georgy gives a mental shrug. If she doesn't go of her own free will then she must be made to leave some other way. She gives it one more try.

'Have you thought of trying to contact Evan?' she asks.

Clarissa stares at her in surprise. 'But how could I?' she asks indignantly. 'I never heard from him once. Not once. Nothing at all. You'd have thought he would have sent a little note after . . . afterwards. Well, wouldn't you?'

Georgy pretends to debate this interesting question. 'Well, it would have been a bit difficult with Thomas around,' she says thoughtfully. 'And it must have been rather hurtful for him, mustn't it?'

'Must it?' asks Clarissa dopily. 'Why?'

Georgy inhales deeply through her nose and smiles at her best friend. 'Well, planning to pass his child over to Thomas without a by-your-leave. He was pretty cut up about it, if you

must know. He was probably heart-broken to know that it's
. . . well, you know.'

Clarissa goggles at her. 'I never thought about that,' she
says slowly.

'And then his wife going off with that man,' continues
Georgy relentlessly. 'He made no effort to stop her. You
know what I think?'

'No,' says Clarissa predictably. 'What?'

'I think,' says Georgy weightily, 'that he was hoping that
you'd chuck Thomas up and go off with him.'

Clarissa sits quite still. She is suddenly remembering how
she sat in this very seat with Evan's arm about her whilst he
told her that she could choose between Thomas and himself.
She remembers how much she loved him at that moment
and how he had likened her to his wife, throwing him over
once she was pregnant . . .

Georgy watches her narrowly, trying to guess at her
thoughts, suspecting a secret.

'Oh,' wails Clarissa. 'Oh dear. Oh what shall I do?'

Georgy smiles to herself. Things are moving very nicely.

'You could try to get in touch with him,' she says casually.
'Try directory enquiries. Perhaps the aunts know. He might
have left a forwarding address. I think he went out of pique.
You used him, well we all did in one way or another, and as
soon as he'd done his work here and Thomas arrived we just
forgot all about him.'

Clarissa is horrified. Her loving feelings for Evan have come
rushing back and she recalls how sweet he was . . . but how
on earth could she achieve such a change? Does she really
want to give up everything for a divorced man with very little
money and a much-loved grown-up daughter?

Seeing that she is wavering, Georgy steps in.

'Think about it,' she says quickly, resolving to remind
Clarissa of Evan at every opportunity and wondering what

went on between them at the end. 'Let's have a drink, shall we?'

'Yes, of course,' says Clarissa mechanically. 'Why not? Oh, perhaps one of us had better see if Thomas would like one.'

Georgy smiles to herself. She notices the indifference as to which of them should offer to help Thomas along to the drawing-room. At the beginning of the conversation the proprietorial note had been very much in evidence. As usual, she has managed to put her friend off balance and she is delighted with the result. She has regained the ground she lost by being careless. Nevertheless, she has no intention of making the same mistake again.

'Up to you,' she says lightly, clinking about at the drinks tray. 'I'll go if you like. Or I can do the drinks . . .'

'Oh, you go,' says Clarissa, taking the easy option. 'I still get a bit tired and there are so many steps to negotiate. I'll start the drinks.'

'OK,' sings out Georgy. 'Whichever. Shan't be long.'

Clarissa sets out the glasses, unaware of the rake lounging amiably at her elbow. He always liked the company of pretty women and seems unaccountably attracted to Clarissa. Aunt Olwen, coming in to check on things, glares at him but he is as unrepentant in death as he ever was in life and merely drifts towards the fireplace.

'Feeling better?' asks Aunt Olwen, who has listened to the entire conversation through the door. 'You are? Yes? Good.'

Her eyes are bright and cold and Clarissa feels an odd sensation, as if she is being assessed.

'Yes,' she mumbles, confused by all that has happened with Georgy, not knowing what she wants or how to attain it.

'Let me do that,' says Aunt Olwen, taking the gin bottle from Clarissa's nerveless fingers. 'You still need to rest. Sit down by the fire and I'll bring you a delicious drink. You'd like that? You would? Good girl.'

The words are comfortingly familiar yet there is something

missing. Worried, Clarissa wanders back and sits down on the sofa, listening for the sound of Thomas's wheelchair. When he and Georgy arrive she observes them closely but she can see now that her fears were quite imaginary. Georgy sets the chair so that Thomas can swing himself on to the sofa beside his wife but it is clear that there is nothing but a kind of camaraderie between them. Clarissa realises that her emotions have been playing tricks on her but now, contrarily, she rather wishes there *had* been something so that she could feel a little less guilty about Evan. Looking at Thomas she sees that he does look old, his face in repose is set and grim and he is quite grey around the temples. She tells herself that this is distinguished but finds herself thinking of Evan and his long legs and bright, fair hair.

Discomfited she smiles quickly at Thomas and catches Georgy's eye. Her best friend raises her glass and sends a tiny encouraging wink. Gratefully Clarissa nods back. Whatever will she do without Georgy? Impossible to imagine; she must beg her to stay on a little longer and rely on her good nature and generosity to help her out of this new, terrible dilemma.

20

As the aunts watch the relationship between Georgy and Thomas with interest, noting Clarissa's growing discontent, they are increasingly conscious of the newcomer in their midst. She is there again this morning, standing, at the end of the drive, half hidden by the oak trees, camouflaged by the shadows. As she stares at the house her attitude is one of eagerness and longing; a desperate hunger emanates from her still, tensely focused figure. The milk van comes rattling down the lane and she turns aside swiftly, melting into the darkness of the woods.

Both Gwyneth and Olwen have seen her. Her brooding presence has alerted these two aged guardians: the present custodians of the house. From their rooms on the first floor, standing well back from the mullioned windows lest they be seen, they watch her. Their thoughts reach out to her, like invisible probes, testing and questioning. They see her disappear amongst the trees and smile gently to themselves.

Clarissa does not see her at all. She sees only the dappled shade, the gleam of the sun through the bare branches, the shadows moving on the drive; all her thoughts are turned inwards. Her face is set in unhappy lines; her arms are folded beneath her breast, hands gripping elbows.

'It isn't fair,' she mutters. 'It simply isn't *fair*.'

The clear, regular note of a bell is carried on the breeze,

across the fields and into the valleys. It is time for Terce at the convent on the hill. Gwyneth and Olwen move uneasily, frowning at the pure, high call to prayer and Clarissa sighs as she turns away from the window. It is too late now to talk to Thomas about Megan's obsession with the nuns. Easter is past and very soon she will enter the convent as a postulant whilst she, Clarissa, will be left in this old house, miles from civilisation, with only a cripple and two old women for companionship.

'It isn't fair!' cries Clarissa – and Olwen and Gwyneth, pausing outside her bedroom door to listen, nod wisely to each other, recognising the note of frustration in her voice.

They make no effort to help or comfort her now. She must go willingly, longingly, not wishing to return, and they are prepared to wait until she has reached the state where flight is her only desire. Slowly, very slowly, they have withdrawn their affection, so that she is left isolated, yet still she will not make a move. Her attempts to find Evan have been pathetic; she does not know his address and therefore cannot trace him by telephone and the office is closed, his flat empty. Even Georgy, who is longing to see her gone, cannot quite think how he can be found. She has suggested a trip to Malvern, perhaps she might see him by chance in the town, but Clarissa cannot bestir herself to such effort. Anyway, what might he think to find her searching for him so blatantly? She has her pride.

'*Not for much longer,*' thinks Georgy grimly, surveying her dispassionately. She is beginning to think that she must resort to her final weapon. She has hoped to avoid it but it is clear that Clarissa is leaving her no alternative. This opinion is underlined after a conversation with Thomas.

'I expect you'll be leaving us soon,' he says cheerfully, one morning at breakfast. 'Didn't you say something about having to be somewhere else just after Easter?'

Georgy remembers it well – too well. She'd said it in the

hope that she might bounce Thomas into some reaction. Well, now she has. It is Clarissa who comes to her defence. Until she has made up her mind – that is to say until someone else has made it up for her and then acted upon it – she needs Georgy at hand.

'Oh you can't leave us just yet,' she cries hastily. 'The spring and early summer is just so perfect here. All the little lambs and things. She must stay mustn't she?'

She looks round the table, appealing to the aunts who are very ready to agree. They sense that it is Georgy who is about to do their dirty work for them. Thomas, who doesn't care too much either way, smiles politely. If Georgy can put off her other commitments, and his wife wishes her to stay, who is he to argue? Georgy is disappointed at his lukewarm response. She knows that if she could shift Clarissa, who has been turning more and more to Thomas since the aunts' subtle defection, she could make him need her.

'I must admit this place has spoiled me,' she says aloud, knowing that the way to Thomas's heart is through admiration of his house and land. 'It's going to be a very difficult act to follow.'

Thomas smiles warmly upon her and her resolve hardens. In this one moment she decides that she will wait no longer. She will play her trump card and stake her future on it.

'Anyone feel like a walk?' she asks brightly, pushing back her chair. She knows that Clarissa always prefers to stuff indoors unless the weather is much warmer than it is on this blowy, capricious, late April morning. Thomas, on the other hand likes to be outside whenever possible.

'I should love it,' he says at once. 'What about it, darling?'

Darling! Georgy grits her teeth and attempts to look encouragingly at Clarissa. Silently, hands clenched, still smiling, she wills her to refuse and a tiny silence falls. The aunts are watching Georgy, their grey eyes calculating, their senses alert, and a cold air seems to drift into the warm atmosphere.

'Well,' hesitates Clarissa. She does not wish to go out into the cold windy morning but it looks churlish to refuse so publicly. 'Well . . .'

'I was hoping,' says Aunt Olwen smoothly, 'that I might have Clarissa's help this morning. There is *such* a pile of ironing and no-one does it quite so beautifully as she does. But I don't want to spoil your fun.'

'Of course I'll do the ironing,' says Clarissa readily, delighted at the chance to opt out. She enjoys the soothing, rhythmical movement of ironing, the smell of warm linen, the crackle of folded sheets. The linen-room is cosy, with the big walk-in airing cupboard that takes up one whole wall, and there is a small portable radio to keep one amused whilst working. 'You don't mind, darling?'

'I quite see that work must come first,' says Thomas, not in the least distressed. 'So, then . . . ?'

He looks enquiringly at Georgy who shrugs humorously.

'You'll have to put up with me, I'm afraid,' she says.

'Wrap up warm,' advises Aunt Gwyneth. 'The wind's chilly. Don't be deceived by the sunshine.'

Georgy pauses by the folly: an oddly roofed, wooden structure, with walls on three sides and a long bench seat. Open to the front, which faces south, it is set on a grassy rise overlooking the lake. She pushes the chair into the shelter of the folly, turns it so that Thomas can see out and then fiddles in the bag which swings from the handle.

'Coffee,' says Thomas, sniffing luxuriously. '*What* a clever girl it is. The aunts are right, it's none too warm. Especially when you can't move about.'

'Poor Thomas,' says Georgy lightly. 'It is *the* most beastly luck. Here warm your hands on this.'

'Bone china, too,' marvels Thomas, admiring the mug. 'Not just plastic.'

'Only the best,' says Georgy in the same light tone. 'What a view!'

Thomas sits silently, surveying his land, and his expression becomes remote and bleak. Sitting on the bench very slightly to the rear of his chair, Georgy watches his profile. She waits until she is certain that his thoughts are dark and bitter before she speaks.

'I want to say something before I leave this place,' she says quietly. 'Forgive me for mentioning it, it's probably frightfully bad form and all that, but I think you are absolutely fantastic. The way you've taken these blows is just breathtaking. I am full of admiration for you and I think Clarissa is the luckiest woman alive. And after the way she's behaved . . .' She pauses as though lost for words, watching Thomas out of the corner of her eye, seeing a new tenseness, a raising of the chin as his brows together, puzzled.

'After the way she's behaved?' he queries slowly.

'I know she's my oldest friend,' says Georgy rapidly, with a kind of breathless indignation, 'but I simply have to say it. I'm ashamed of her. And when I think of all you've given her and what you were going through . . . I sometimes feel quite speechless with rage. Not one man in a million would have been so generous. And especially . . .' She pauses, sniffing as though she is close to tears, and touches his rigid shoulder briefly. 'Sorry. I just had to say it. I know I'm speaking out of turn and you're probably disgusted with me. I know it sounds disloyal but it's been too much to hold in, somehow. Forgive me. I expect you'd like to go back now?'

There is a long, long silence. Georgy has an odd feeling that someone is watching her and she twists to peer out, praying that Clarissa hasn't changed her mind and followed them. The grounds are empty. When she looks back at Thomas she experiences a shock. His grey eyes are cold, his mouth grim. He looks quite changed and she knows a moment of fear.

'What do you mean?' he asks. '"After the way she's behaved"?'

Georgy swallows, crosses her fingers beneath her thighs and throws caution to the winds.

'Well, you know! About the baby,' she says, almost impatiently. 'Being unfaithful while you were stuck in hospital. Honestly. How could she? The callous disloyalty of it. And then pretending the baby was yours! I couldn't believe it when she told me. Of course, she was out of her mind by the time I got here. That's why she sent for me. I dropped everything of course. My new job in America. New boyfriend.' She shrugs. 'But that's not important. It's what friendship's all about, isn't it? I'm not surprised she lost the baby. When she was told you were coming home early, she was scared out of her wits.'

Thomas stares at her and her heart hammers with terror. There is something seriously scary about him and she swallows nervously.

'And what if she hadn't lost the baby?' he asks gently.

'Look,' says Georgy, twisting her hands in her lap, 'I don't know if I should tell you all this. Promise you won't let me down?' He nods unsmilingly and she hurries on. 'Well, we were going to pretend it was mine . . .'

Carefully, utterly absolving the aunts of knowledge or blame – she will need them later – she proceeds to weave a rope for Clarissa's neck. Thomas sits quite still, and in silence, until she has finished.

'I see,' he says, after she has stumbled to a halt. He hands her the mug. 'Take me back, please.'

'Please,' cries Georgy, nearly in tears, quite genuine ones this time. What will she do if Thomas betrays her? She feels frightened, excited and emotional, all at the same time. 'Wait. I've done something terrible, haven't I? I thought you knew. She agreed that she would tell you the truth when she lost it and decided to stay with you after all . . . Oh, *God*! What shall I do? And I agreed to be party to her deception . . .'

'You have acted out of friendship,' says Thomas quietly. 'I shan't let you down, I promise.'

'But how . . . ? I mean, what will you say?' Georgy's anxiety is unfeigned. She really wants to know how Thomas is going to deal with his wife without dropping Clarissa's really, *really* best friend right in the shit.

'I shall say that the doctor is suspicious,' says Thomas calmly. 'I shall confront her with his suspicions and see what she says.'

Georgy looks at him, silent with admiration. This quality of deviousness is almost in her own class and she sees that she must be cautious in future.

'But why now?' she asks, concerned lest there might be a flaw in this excellent plan and wanting him to be aware of any weaknesses. 'I mean it's nearly four months ago . . . *Was* the doctor suspicious?'

'It was a very confusing business,' says Thomas thoughtfully. 'He came to give me a check-up yesterday. How fortuitous. I shall say that the subject came up again.'

He broods for a moment and Georgy, carried away by this unexpected stroke of genius on Thomas's part, pulls herself together. She was almost on the point of giving him some advice on how to put the frighteners on Clarissa.

'I expect you'll want me to go?' she suggests in a small voice, putting away the coffee things.

'Not just yet,' he says – but he is preoccupied and she can take no real comfort from his words. At least he does not seem to blame or despise her. With a huge, private sigh of relief, Georgy begins the long push back to the house.

The aunts are waiting for them, eager, watchful, sly.

'Where's Clarissa?' asks Thomas, almost casually.

Above his head they exchange a long, telling look with

Georgy who, to her amazement, is aware of their partisan-ship. Her heart rises as they smile and she turns away to hide the exultation in her face. She has nothing more to fear. There is no doubt that, confronted by Thomas in his present mood, Clarissa will admit everything.

21

Clarissa does indeed admit everything. In her present state of confusion, misery and indecision, she breaks down at once. It is a noisy, messy business and her wailing can be heard all over the house. Luckily, her admission is so broken with shrieks and cries that nothing is terribly clear except the one vital, overwhelming fact. She is guilty. Before she can admit to anything too damaging to anyone else, the aunts remove her. She is taken away, sobbing and protesting and nearly hysterical. The aunts fuss over her just as they did in the good old days and she allows herself to be undressed and put to bed. Fortunately a calming cordial is prepared and ready at hand and gradually her sobs are quietened until at last she falls into a deep, drugged sleep.

Georgy stays well out of the way and Thomas does not appear for lunch. He remains in his rooms, silent with mortification and rage. He has lost his manhood twice over. Aunt Olwen goes to him with a cup of nourishing soup and a chicken sandwich but he pushes them aside untouched. Looking at him, Aunt Olwen sees for the first time his likeness to dear Mama. The resemblance is uncanny – and most encouraging. She knows that he is moving towards a vital moment in the history of the house and it seems as if he will be ready to accept it.

'I can hardly believe it,' he mutters – and she clucks

181 •

sympathetically as she moves about, tidying and making his room comfortable and warm. 'She deceived us all,' he says bitterly.

Aunt Olwen sighs regretfully, lips pursed as she shakes her head at the shocking ways of humankind.

'What shall I do?' he murmurs.

She guesses that this is a rhetorical question but decides to attempt a touch of guidance, to give a positive direction to his thoughts. 'I have a feeling that she will not stay with us long, my dear boy,' she says gently. 'She has never fitted in, you know. We've all tried very hard to make her welcome, to be one of the family, but she does not belong here. We were all taken in by her manner, and she is charming in many ways, but . . .' She lets the 'but' linger regretfully for a second or two. 'Forgive me for saying these things about your wife . . .'

He presses her hand speakingly, gratefully. He has been a fool, this is clear, but, as usual, the darling old aunts are letting him off the hook, taking his mistake to themselves, viewing it as a family problem.

'Of course,' says Aunt Olwen doubtfully, 'if you still want her . . .'

'No,' says Thomas strongly. 'No. But what can we do? I can't throw her out.'

She is disappointed to see evidence of such weak foolishness still lingering in his new, harder character but she is patient. She has it all planned.

'I think that she will go of her own accord,' she says, patting his arm. 'Trust me. It will be all for the best. It was an unfortunate mistake. Perfectly understandable. You were grieving for poor, darling Claerwen and I understand this sort of thing often happens at those times when a man's resistance is low. Women are cunning, clever creatures.'

Thomas does not deny this – and why should he? He is surrounded by them – but merely nods miserably.

Aunt Olwen sees a case of self-pity coming on and becomes brisker. 'I think you should stay in your rooms for a day or two whilst things are sorted out,' she says thoughtfully. 'Clarissa must go. And Georgy, too,' she adds sharply. She pauses but Thomas does not protest. She nods, satisfied. Georgy has done her work and there is no further use for her but her suspicions must not be raised just yet. Clarissa must be dealt with first . . . 'All will be well, dear boy,' says Aunt Olwen. 'Now drink your soup.'

'Thanks,' he says moodily. 'Thanks, aunt. It's just that I feel such a frightful fool.'

'Nonsense,' she says robustly. 'These girls are not our kind. The house – we – need our own people about us. Now I shall be back in ten minutes and I want to see all that lunch eaten up.'

Thomas sighs heavily but he sips at the soup which is very tasty and, to his surprise he finishes it to the last drop. By the time he has eaten his sandwich he can barely keep his eyes open.

'Reaction,' he tells himself, yawning. 'Well, it's to only to be expected . . .'

It occurs to him that he was surprisingly ready to believe Georgy's revelations, that out there by the folly some sixth sense seemed to crystallise his mind, helping him to think with a quite frightening clarity. It was as if someone were hovering near . . .

When she comes creeping in some time later, Aunt Olwen finds him asleep and snoring. Placing a rug gently round him, she collects up his plates and tiptoes quietly out.

For a few days a silence hangs over the house. Oddly, both Thomas and Clarissa sleep a great deal and, when they wake, feel heavy-headed and lethargic, quite unable to confront the problems which face them. On the third morning, however, Clarissa wakes to a sense of doom, untinged with soothing haziness. She remembers everything and hugs herself in fear. Before she can get up and go to find Georgy – surely her really, *really* best friend will help her? – Aunt Gwyneth appears with a delicious breakfast on a tray.

'We were thinking,' she says kindly, arranging a shawl about Clarissa's shoulders. 'We think that you need a little change. We all need time to adjust and we thought that you might like a trip to the town. Aunt Olwen has some shopping to do and you could have lunch in our little café. Best to keep out of the way at present, wouldn't you say?'

'Oh yes,' cries Clarissa gratefully. 'Oh dear . . .'

'Now, now. No tears. Least said, soonest mended. You eat up your breakfast and get dressed. We'll be ready when you are.'

'Is Georgy coming?' asks Clarissa eagerly, picking up her coffee cup. She longs for a chat with her best friend. There is so much to say; so much to be sorted out. How can she manage without Georgy's advice?

'I think *not*,' says Aunt Gwyneth gently. 'Poor Georgy isn't too well. A dreadful migraine. She's sleeping in this morning.' And so she is – very heavily indeed. 'Plenty of time for chats later. A change of scene will do you good. Now, not too long.'

As Clarissa eats her egg she feels almost as if Aunt Gwyneth is behaving just as she did before Thomas came back. At the thought of him – his icy rage, his terrifying eyes so fierce and cold, his cruel words – she feels terror rising again but she pushes it down as best she can. She will not think of it this morning, not until she has seen Georgy . . .

It is a fine spring morning, although the wind is still cold, and Aunt Gwyneth tucks her tenderly into the passenger seat whilst Aunt Olwen climbs in and starts the car. They hardly speak during the journey. Clarissa stares out at the now-familiar countryside remembering other happier trips. On the steep hillsides the lambs gambol with their staid mothers, the hedges are faintly flushed with new, bright green and the sky is a pure and tender blue. Clarissa swallows tearfully as she thinks of how she has messed things up and she longs for a kind word and a friendly touch. Aunt Olwen's driving seems more than usually erratic this morning, however, and Clarissa is afraid to distract her by having a weeping fit or asking her advice. She remembers how she laughed over 'the quick and the dead' joke and feels that it was a world away from her present misery.

When they arrive at the café, to have some coffee before embarking on the shopping, Aunt Olwen gives a little cry of annoyance; she has left the shopping list in the car. Clarissa's offer to fetch it is refused and she is sent in to find a table whilst Aunt Olwen goes back to the car. Clarissa blinks as she comes in out of the bright sunshine, peering about her for a vacant table. Suddenly a man rises from a seat near the window and Clarissa gives a muffled cry. It is Evan.

He takes her quickly by the arm, turning her away from interested stares, making her sit down. She stares at him, with wide, frightened eyes; she had forgotten how fair he is, how handsome, how comforting.

'Evan,' she murmurs shakily as he slips an arm about her shoulders and presses his lips to her hair – lank and smelly after several days in bed, unfortunately, but he rises above it – and whispers to her.

'Cariad,' he says, 'oh, how wonderful to see you again. I've missed you so much.'

Cariad? She leans back within his arm to stare at him in surprise and he smiles down at her.

'But you disappeared,' she wails quietly – because of the other customers – but pitifully. 'Why didn't you write to me?'

'But cariad,' he says again – he's never called her that before and she likes it – 'you never wrote to me, either. Not a line or a phone call. I was so sad about the baby but even then there was no word from you. The aunts told me you were ill and I felt so helpless. So excluded. As the weeks passed I thought you'd decided to choose your husband. How could I contact you with Thomas there? I might have got you into terrible trouble and I thought that I'd done you quite enough harm as it was.'

At this exhibition of true, unselfish love, the tears brim over and slide down her cheeks.

'Oh, Evan,' she whispers, kissing his hand over and over again. 'Oh, the most ghastly thing has happened. You'll never guess.'

'What is it?' he asks, looking stern and manly. 'Has someone been upsetting you?'

Her lips shake as she thinks how hardly used she has been and she cannot speak for several moments. He pats her tenderly. The waitress approaches looking anxious and Evan nods, concerned but indicating that coffee should be brought.

'Thomas has found out,' Clarissa tells him, finding her voice at last. She stares up at him with tragic eyes. 'The doctor suspected something was not quite right when I . . . when I, you know, miscarried. He mentioned it again to Thomas a few days ago and Thomas demanded to know the truth. Honestly, Evan, he was *terrifying*.'

Fortunately, the coffee arrives at this moment and Evan is spared any noble promises of revenge. As Clarissa pours the coffee with trembling hands, Evan sees Aunt Olwen peering through the glass door. He raises his hand behind Clarissa's back and waggles his fingers, signalling success. Aunt Olwen bustles in and stands beside them.

'Well,' she says with every evidence of amazement. 'Evan! Now this *is* a surprise.'

'A pleasant one, I hope,' he says, rising courteously to his feet and pulling out a chair. 'I had some business to wind up in the town and decided to have some coffee here, for old time's sake.'

'Isn't it an amazing coincidence?' asks Clarissa, looking with drowned but happy eyes at Aunt Olwen.

'Amazing,' agrees Aunt Olwen blandly, beaming at her. 'Just what the doctor ordered by the look of you.'

Clarissa beams back, remembering how jolly the dear old aunts have always been in the past about little indiscretions, and meanwhile holding Evan's hand very tightly in her own.

'It seems to me,' says Evan firmly, 'that it's time you made that choice, Clarissa. You can't leave me hanging on again without a word. Do you want to stay with Thomas or will you come with me? I have the dearest little house in Malvern. Warm and cosy it is, not what you've been used to, I know, but I think you'll be happy there.'

There is a silence. Clarissa thinks of the long dark passages and draughty landings; of being alone with her nightmares once Georgy has gone and Megan has entered the convent; of the quick and the dead who inhabit the shadowy rooms. She remembers the look on Thomas's face and shudders; she knows, too, that even the darling old aunts can become withdrawn and unfriendly. How lonely she will be with not even the hope of children. Surely, away from the influence of the dead and without fear, she will conceive normal, happy children?

Both Evan and Aunt Olwen are counting on it; future guardians and custodians will appear in due course, raised in love and harmony and introduced to their inheritance at the proper moment. This time there will be no false starts, no terrors, no mistakes – and no interference.

'Well,' says Evan gently, lovingly, 'which is it to be?'

Even now she dithers; how is it to be arranged and who will tell Thomas? At the thought of such an interview she feels weak with fright.

'Do you know,' Aunt Olwen is saying thoughtfully, 'I

think that the two of you should go now. Right away. Don't hesitate. Don't look back. I feel that you two belong together. And Thomas will never forgive you, either of you, you know. He will soon find out who your lover is, if he doesn't know already, and the divorce will be a painful business. Thomas can be quite implacable.'

Clarissa shudders again; this she can believe. 'But how can we?' she asks, longing to be let off so freely, without explanations. 'Oh, if only we could.'

'You can,' says Aunt Olwen firmly. 'It will be all for the best. No more scenes and recriminations. Quick, sharp action is best in these cases. We'll send your things on after you.'

'But what about Georgy?' cries Clarissa. 'What will she think if I don't come home? How shall I explain to her?'

'I think that you should forget about Georgy for the present,' says Aunt Olwen. 'She is dangerous.'

'Dangerous?' repeats Clarissa, disbelievingly. 'Whatever do you mean? How can Georgy be dangerous?'

'Poor girl,' says Aunt Olwen, patting Clarissa's hand. 'So trusting. So loyal. It distresses me to have to tell you this but it was she who told Thomas, not the doctor. She would like to be Thomas's wife. She betrayed you.'

'*Georgy* told him?' whispers Clarissa. 'Oh, I don't believe it.'

'It's true,' says Aunt Olwen. 'She will not win him, however. He does not care for her and we shall not allow it, you may be sure of that. But do not trust her again. I shouldn't invite her to your little nest.'

Clarissa shakes her head, dumb with shock, remembering how she suspected Georgy of playing up to Thomas – and to Evan. She holds Evan's hand even more tightly, her thoughts reeling.

'Forget it all,' counsels Evan, arm about her. 'Put it behind you. Come with me to my little house in Malvern. We shall be happy together there.'

'But what will Angharad say?' asks Clarissa anxiously. 'Supposing she doesn't like me?'

Evan and Aunt Olwen exchange a glance.

'Angharad won't be with us,' Evan tells her.

'Aah,' says Aunt Olwen, alert. 'She is taking up the position we spoke of earlier?'

'Soon now,' he answers. 'Very soon. One or two things still to be ironed out . . .'

'A position?' asks Clarissa. 'Has she got a nursing job?'

'Angharad has done very well,' says Evan, smiling to himself. 'She's had the offer of private nursing. It's a very good job which allows her to use her many talents. Nursing, cooking, house-keeping . . . Oh, many, many things. She won't be too far away so we shall see her now and then.'

'I'd hate to put her nose out of joint,' explains Clarissa. 'If you think she'll understand . . .'

'Angharad knows all about it,' Evan reassures her, still smiling. 'We have her blessing.'

'Excellent,' beams Aunt Olwen, relieved. 'So . . . ?'

They both look at Clarissa knowing that it is now or never. She must be forced to the decision which she will never have the courage to take for herself. Clarissa takes a deep breath and makes up her mind.

'I shall come with you, Evan,' she says.

'There must be no second thoughts,' warns Aunt Olwen. 'No running back to Thomas. He will never countenance another humiliation. I shall deal with everything, have no fear, and Aunt Gwyneth and I shall come to visit you, but I must have your word that there will be no looking back.'

'No looking back,' agrees Clarissa, smiling at Evan – though she is still shocked about Georgy. 'This is forever. I just feel it.'

Aunt Olwen and Evan exchange another glance. 'Forever,' they repeat, smiling triumphantly at each other.

22

Georgy can hardly believe her luck when she hears the news. That Clarissa should remove herself from the lists so quickly is a tremendous relief. At the same time, she cannot help feeling just the least bit irritated that she has had the good fortune to fall on her feet. Aunt Olwen has told her the truth – that Clarissa met up quite by chance with Evan and has run off with him – but she makes it clear that she does not wish Thomas to know the name of Clarissa's lover.

There is something in the way in which she imparts this instruction that makes Georgy very slightly nervous. It is clear that her future in the house depends very largely on the dear old aunts and she hastens to give her word. She is glad that Thomas has never asked for information on this point and that she has not felt it necessary to tell him. She can assure the aunts with confidence that she will never mention the subject again. There is, however, a reticence about disclosing to her Clarissa's whereabouts which Georgy decides to dismiss as unnecessary caution. She has no doubt that she will hear soon enough from her very best friend and she willingly packs up Clarissa's things which the aunts take away to be sent on. She does not press them for information; she needs their goodwill. Meanwhile she goes to work on Thomas.

When the aunts break the news to him, Thomas's feelings

are very similar to Georgy's. He feels a tremendous relief when he realises that there will be no more unpleasant, messy scenes but he is annoyed that Clarissa has got off so lightly without any further punishment. The aunts, however, persuade him that he is very lucky and encourage him in his declarations that he will divorce her as soon as it can be arranged. They suspect – quite rightly – that he will be in no hurry to discuss his affairs with anyone just yet, nor do they wish him to be free too soon. Nevertheless, they are quite intelligent enough to realise that to attempt to stop him would merely strengthen his resolve. Let him rage about Clarissa's infidelity and talk of dragging her name through the courts. It is getting the whole business out of his system very nicely. They are too busy wondering how to dislodge Georgy to have time to fret too much about Thomas.

Georgy has no intention of being dislodged but she is dismayed at Thomas's lack of response to her warm sympathy and womanly wiles. Naturally, she doesn't expect a sexual interest to be shown in her, she guesses that dear old Thomas was never much of a one for the physical aspects of married life, but she has hoped for much more of a reaction by now. She is beginning to suspect that Clarissa was a novelty to Thomas; that he was attracted to her simply because she was so different to anything he had experienced and she was able to sweep him off his feet without really having to work at it. She remembers how Clarissa complained of his sexual indifference, his lack of interest in a social life, his middle-aged dullness, and she sees that she has her work cut out. Moreover, the aunts make no attempt to encourage or help her. They have withdrawn and are no longer cosy, jolly old dears. Instead, they are watchful, cool, inaccessible. She becomes impatient, pacing her bedroom floor as she thinks of ways to ingratiate herself with Thomas and with the aunts before her time runs out.

It is Thomas himself who brings matters to a head. He has

no thoughts of Georgy as a future wife but he realises how very useful she is to him as a nurse and companion. He is aware that the aunts are no longer strong enough to push him about the grounds; to drive him around, hauling the wheelchair in and out of the car; to keep him amused, drinking and chatting late into the night when he cannot sleep. Georgy is thin and wiry and strong and makes light of the physical problems of his life. It occurs to him that, although he would rather have the house to himself – he includes the aunts in 'himself' – nevertheless, he must accept the fact that he needs assistance of some kind. After all, poor Georgy has been left in the lurch – abandoned by Clarissa, having given up job and boyfriend to rush to her assistance – and now has to start her life all over again.

He drops his bombshell one morning at breakfast, over the kedgeree.

'I expect you'll be thinking of leaving us now,' he says to Georgy, 'but I have to admit that I'm wondering what on earth I shall do without you.'

There is a moment of utter silence. The aunts and Georgy sit quite still, electrified by this totally unexpected admission.

Thomas ploughs on with his kedgeree, unaware of the sensation he has caused.

'I'm sure you don't want to become a nursemaid to a crippled old man,' he says, laughing lightly at such a silly suggestion, 'but I'd certainly offer you the job if you were to apply for it.'

In truth, he is only half serious. He hasn't really thought it through and, anyway, he doesn't expect Georgy to accept. Why should a bright intelligent girl want to shut herself away with two old women and a cripple? He has underestimated Georgy, however, who sees her chance and seizes it. To be made such an offer, in front of the aunts, is a stroke of the most amazing luck.

'And I should be delighted to accept it,' she says boldly,

smiling sweetly at Thomas. 'As you know, I rather burned my bridges so as to come here to Clarissa and I don't quite know where I shall go or what I'll do now. I have no family and few friends. No one who really cares about me . . . Apart from Clarissa, that is. Or at least I thought so until she went off without a word. Anyway, apart from anything else, I've become so terribly fond of you all. It's as if you *are* my family, now. I'd miss you dreadfully if I had to go away.'

She laughs a little deprecatingly, mocking herself for such sentimental nonsense, whilst peeping slyly at the aunts to note their reaction. They look so stunned that she wants to burst out laughing.

'*Got 'em!*' she thinks with fierce delight.

'Well,' Thomas is saying, rather taken aback by such a prompt response and laughing foolishly. 'Well . . .'

He looks at the aunts, realising that he has probably jumped the gun, seeing a distinct lack of warmth on their jolly old faces.

'It is very sweet of Georgy,' begins Aunt Gwyneth carefully, 'to be so generous but . . .'

'Oh, no,' bursts in Georgy girlishly. She is beginning to really enjoy herself now, knowing that Thomas cannot possibly retract without losing a great deal of face. 'Oh, not at all generous. I should be so happy to stay and be useful . . .'

'*But,*' continues Aunt Gwyneth indomitably, 'I do wonder if we need someone more qualified? Someone used to lifting patients, perhaps? Or . . .'

'Good heavens,' says Thomas irritably, put out by this slur on his masculinity. 'I'm not *quite* helpless, aunt. I can do most things for myself . . .'

'Absolutely,' interjects Georgy quietly but strongly – and Thomas sends her a grateful glance.

'Well,' says Aunt Olwen, who sees that they are merely antagonising Thomas and will get nowhere. 'It certainly is a most interesting thought. I had no idea, Thomas, that you felt you needed someone to entertain you on a full-time basis.'

This is a clever remark which makes Thomas feel rather like a child in need of a nanny. Georgy is too quick for them, however. She sees where Aunt Olwen is leading and hurries into the breach.

'Thomas doesn't need a nurse,' she says confidently. 'He manages terribly well. He needs a strong, young companion. Someone to help with the wheelchair, drive him about – although there is no reason why he shouldn't have a specially adapted car in due course – and just be around for him. All I'm saying is, if that's what he wants and he thinks I can supply it, then I'd be very honoured to accept his sweet offer.' She pushes back her chair and stands up. 'Weren't we going down to Home Farm?' she asks Thomas cheerfully.

'Heavens, yes,' he says with palpable relief, throwing down his napkin. 'I'd completely forgotten. You see?' he appeals to the aunts, laughingly. 'She's a great secretary, as well.'

They laugh with him and, still smiling, watch Georgy help him back into his wheelchair and push him from the room. Presently there is silence. The aunts' eyes meet, cold and angry. Georgy has jumped the gun, pre-empted their own arrangements, although Thomas's readiness to accept a companion certainly smooths their path . . . Their thoughts run together, considering, rejecting, planning, but one thought is uppermost in their minds; in two days' time it is May Day. No doubt the Goddess will supply an answer. They will need time to summon all their resources but it must be a very special occasion. Strong magic will be necessary to prevent this new disastrous plan.

Georgy has boned up on the old pagan festivals and she is well aware that Beltane is approaching. She has made one or two sorties into the grove in the aunts' absence and although, even in bright sunlight, it is an eerie place she is faintly amused at these two old dears' outdated beliefs. To be honest, she has to admit that the mounds and the evidence of blood on the flat sacrifice stone is decidedly creepy but she really cannot take any of it seriously. She vaguely remembers the nightmare she had when the aunts drugged her but she is now inclined to laugh at the whole business. What with this and the ghosts . . . Well, honestly . . .

Nevertheless, she wonders if there might be a bit of mileage to be made out of it. Although she has reinforced her accept-ance of Thomas's offer so that he cannot possibly back out, she realises just how difficult the two old biddies could make her life. Perhaps if she could find something to hold over them, as it were . . . ?

The idea grows stronger and she broods on it carefully. Although it is essential not to raise the aunts' suspicions she is determined this May Day Eve to neither eat nor drink anything which might conceivably be drugged. She will pay a little midnight visit to the grove and to the site on the hill behind, where clearly there have been fires in the past. She knows that Beltane is one of the fire festivals. Whilst the aunts are away shopping, she follows the path into the woods and maps out a route and a hiding place for herself, so that, wherever they are worshipping, she will be able to follow and watch undetected. She knows that she dare not risk using a torch, so she retraces the path several times, memorising distinctive features as landmarks. Just as she had on the morning in the folly with Thomas, so today she has the feeling that she is being watched, but, turn as quickly as she might, she can see no-one. Laughing at her fancies she returns to the house, prepared and excited. She feels confident that the aunts will not want Thomas to know that they are mad as hatters; will be grateful to have their weird and rather unsavoury habits kept a secret.

The aunts are relieved when Georgy announces that she has

a bad headache after lunch on May Day Eve. They make a nice little cordial for her, which she assures them that she has drunk and enjoyed, and they are not at all surprised when she announces later that afternoon that she will go to bed. Although her headache has eased, she says, she is feeling very tired and she stumbles away to bed, yawning widely. Later, much later, they check on her, but she is curled up into a ball, sleeping heavily, and they smile as they creep away. Georgy gives them ten minutes, counted out slowly and painstakingly second by second, before she rises, dresses warmly and follows them from the house.

As the flickering lanterns guide her through the darkness she has a sense of *déjà vu*. She has been here before at night, with the twigs pulling at her clothes, whipping against her cheeks, although tonight there is no wind. It is mild and still with a moon rising in the east. It is difficult in the dark to follow her prepared route but she does very well whilst she can see the lights. This time she does not intend to stand in the stone circle but plans to hide on the path that leads up to the open hillside where the bonfire waits, piled high with dry brushwood. The air seems full of whispers, of voices that sigh and groan, and she shivers a little, not so confident now, feeling that the invisible inhabitants of the grove might be close at hand. Mist curls about the tree trunks, drifting eerily, obscuring the path, and she stumbles on, reaching out blindly as its chill dankness enfolds her. Now she can see nothing but darkness and the flowing mist and she pauses, peering about her, looking for the landmarks she memorised earlier. The thick, white vapour parts suddenly and she gives a gasping, strangled cry of fright as a long arm reaches out towards her, fingers touching her hair and her mouth. She catches her breath, giving a little sob of relief as she sees that the arm is simply a branch, its fingers are merely twigs.

She stands for a moment, recovering herself, and catches

a glimpse of the lanterns moving away to her right in the darkness. She moves slowly forward, her eyes fixed on the brightness which glows amongst the trees but as she does so she is convinced that something or someone is moving with her, at a distance but keeping parallel with her. She knows now that she has missed the path and is deep in the grove and she stops, pressing herself close to a tree trunk as she stares about her, big-eyed with terror as she tries to see her pursuer . . .

The scream freezes the life in her body so that she remains quite still, eyes closed now, biting her trembling lips. Slowly she inches round the trunk and, still sheltering beside the ancient oak, she sees the dark hooded shapes bowing before the slab, arms raised, the glint of light on metal, and she waits instinctively for the sharp, thin animal cry which she remembers from her dream.

She is prepared for the second scream but now she becomes aware again of the powerful and terrifying presence of her pursuer. She has forgotten that she once thought that these rites were amusing and her heart thuds in her side and her throat is dry. The presence is moving closer, she sees the movement of its shadow and her muscles lock rigid in her limbs. She forces herself to move slowly around the tree, feeling the dry, rough bark beneath her flat palms and stretched fingers, willing herself to be ready to run, to fight.

All is silent. She stands quite still, listening intently, feeling an easing of tension. Taking a deep, shaking breath she steps away from the tree . . . The figure before her is tall and dark, although, within the folds of the hood, she can see the fierce, cold, terrifying eyes watching her. Georgy opens her mouth but no sound comes. She braces herself, forcing herself to spring forward, but she is seized by two strong hands. She gasps, struggles, but her opponent, still holding her by the arms, shakes her, lifts her easily, lightly, and strikes her head against the gnarled trunk. There is a crack as her neck snaps and she collapses, lifeless, into her killer's arms.

Some moments later the aunts approach the bonfire, bearing their lanterns and the bodies of some luckless small animals. There has been strong magic this night and, as they stand together, they experience the now-familiar sensation of someone else close by; they feel her power, her ruthlessness, and they wonder if their mother is near to them, reincarnated, soon to be restored to them. Quickly they pick up the rags already prepared, soaked with paraffin, and hold them to the lanterns' flame. As they flare up they fling the rags on to the dry wood so that it ignites, burns steadily for a moment and then roars up in a billowing fire of scarlet and gold.

When it seems that Georgy has left them without warning or explanation the aunts are convinced that it is a direct result of their propitiations to the Goddess; She has heard their petitions and answered them swiftly. It is odd that Georgy has taken none of her belongings with her but they have never questioned the ways of their Mistress and they are too relieved that their problems have been solved so promptly and easily to worry about small details. Georgy came from nowhere and has returned from whence she came. The new grave in the deepest, darkest part of the wood is known only to her killer who, having removed the last obstacle to her desires, will soon reveal herself.

Thomas can hardly believe it when the aunts tell him, gently and sympathetically, that Georgy has run out on him. No doubt, they murmur, she felt, on reflection, that the responsibility was too great; that she was too young to tie herself down and she couldn't bring herself to tell him. They mention a telephone call a day or two ago – the aunts' eyes meet and slide away, after all, it might be the truth; they are vague, saying that it was some man who called, some old friend . . . Thomas is resigned. Only Claerwen has been true, devoted and faithful, just as her daughter is to her vocation.

In June, Megan enters the convent as a postulant. She is radiant. She is filled with peace – yet she is aware of a faint undercurrent of unease. She has had a letter from Clarissa, telling her everything, assuring her of her love, requiring her prayers, and Megan is glad, knowing that she is truly safe with Evan. Nevertheless, she is aware of that other presence, dark and terrible, who blocks her Sight, confusing dream with reality. Megan knows that she must become strong; she will put on the whole armour of God; she will grow in her faith, so as to be ready for the future moment when she is matched, as she quite certainly knows she will be, against this powerful, dark force. Meanwhile, she leaves the house in the care of her father and her aunts and embraces her vocation whole-heartedly and with deep joy.

On Midsummer Eve the house is swept and garnished, ready for its new mistress. The aunts wait, knowing that today she who has been watching and waiting will show herself at last. As the evening shadows draw across the lawn and the sky flames and burns in the west she comes on long strong legs, her fair hair bundled into a braid down her back. Her grey eyes flicker and shine, like bright light striking cold sea water; her cruel, narrow mouth smiles to see the aged guardians, the custodians awaiting her. As she approaches they hold their breath. Truly their mother has been reincarnated, has returned to them in their hour of need. They hold out their hands to her and she sweeps triumphantly inside with them, entering in at last to the house she has coveted and watched for so many months.

'Welcome!' they cry tremulously, shaken by her revealed strength, recognising her ruthless power with trepidation. 'Welcome Angharad, niece and kinswoman.'

She laughs at them, privately delighting in their barely concealed fear, eager to take up the work prepared for her; work far more important than the role of nurse, cook, companion, for which dear Thomas has so obligingly paved the way. He, too, must welcome her, falling victim to her charms and spells, until he feels that nothing should be withheld from her, that she is a second daughter to him. She embraces the aunts, kissing them warmly, seducing them back into loving submission, stilling their fear.

'You are my family,' she whispers, 'all of you.'

And she raises her arms to summon the inhabitants of the house, not only the quick but also the dead, who rise up out of the shadows to greet her.

A selection of bestsellers by Willa Marsh

Sisters Under the Skin	0 340 70798 4	£6.99	☐
Facing the Music	0 340 67477 6	£6.99	☐
Amy Wingate's Journal	0 340 67475 X	£6.99	☐

A selection of bestsellers by her *alter ego*, Marcia Willett

Looking Forward	0 7472 5996 8	£5.99	☐
Second Time Around	0 7472 5716 7	£5.99	☐
Starting Over	0 7472 5428 1	£6.99	☐
Hattie's Mill	0 7472 5427 3	£5.99	☐
The Dipper	0 7472 5202 5	£5.99	☐
The Courtyard	0 7472 5201 7	£5.99	☐
Thea's Parrot	0 7472 4904 0	£5.99	☐
Those Who Serve	0 7472 4869 9	£5.99	☐

All Hodder Headline books are available at your local bookshop or newsagent, or can be ordered direct from the publisher. Just tick the titles you want and fill in the form below. Prices and availability subject to change without notice.

Hodder Headline Books, Cash Sales Department, Bookpoint, 39 Milton Park, Abingdon, OXON, OX14 4TD, UK. E-mail address: order@bookpoint.co.uk. If you have a credit card you may order by telephone – (01235) 400414.

Please enclose a cheque or postal order made payable to Bookpoint Ltd to the value of the cover price and allow the following for postage and packing:
UK & BFPO – £1.00 for the first book, 50p for the second book, and 30p for each additional book ordered up to a maximum charge of £3.00.
OVERSEAS & EIRE – £2.00 for the first book, £1.00 for the second book, and 50p for each additional book.

Name _____

Address_____

_____

_____

If you would prefer to pay by credit card, please complete:
Please debit my Visa/Access/Diner's Card/American Express (delete as applicable) card no:

Signature _____

Expiry Date_____

If you would NOT like to receive further information on our products please tick the box. ☐